JOURNEY TO THE TROPICS

By

Kileen Prather

To: Kathy -
Happy journeys...
Kileen Prather

Journey to the Tropics
by Kileen Prather

Kileenp@gmail.com

Cover Design by Summer R. Morris
Book Layout by Suzanne Austin Wells

Published by
Chauncey Park Press
735 N. Grove Avenue
Oak Park, Illinois 60302

Printed in the United States of America
ISBN: 978-0-9802167-8-3

Author's Note:

This novel is a work of fiction. All of the main characters are fictitious and any resemblance to real persons is purely coincidental. Though settings, buildings, and businesses exist; liberties may have been taken as to their actual location and description. This story has no purpose other than to entertain the reader.

Dedication

To Nancy for all her help with editing. And, to my awesome granddaughter, Isabel; may life bring you all the happiness and treasures you deserve. And to my two wonderful sons, Rick and Frank; may life bless both of you. And, never out of my thoughts, Ray and Tim, my brothers, who are always there for me.

Chapter One

Just what we need, snow, she thought to herself.

When he walked into the hospital waiting room the doctor saw a woman of medium height with shoulder-length dark brown hair turn towards him. She had been staring out the window and as the physician looked in that direction, he saw that she had been watching the snow falling outside. It had been a long winter but now it was late April and spring was blossoming. Although the physician knew the snow would be melted by the next morning, it was still an irritation.

As he refocused on the woman, she turned and looked at him with questions in her eyes. And, oh what eyes. He was startled by her piercing blue eyes which seemed to draw him in. The doctor had been practicing for many years and thought he was pretty much immune to anything after so much tragedy and sorrow. But he heard himself gasp as he looked at her. The blue was like the sky on a bright sunny day and he found it difficult not to stare at the woman standing in front of him.

Quickly regaining control, he addressed her.

"Mrs. Noonan? I am Doctor Fisher."

"It is nice to meet you, Doctor. I know the prognosis is not very good but how is she doing today?"

"Mrs. O'Reilly is not doing well, I am sorry to say. Your mother's white blood cells were so low we had to give her a transfusion before giving the chemo. I know you have been waiting a long time and I just wanted you to know it is still going to be a while. Perhaps you would like to go to the hospital cafeteria. I can let the nurse know where you will be in case you are needed."

"Thank you Doctor. I think I will get some lunch." Sighing Fiona took one last cheerless look at the snow coming down. She followed the physician out of the room and took the elevator down to the hospital cafeteria.

Finding a table near a window in the restaurant and eating her salad she wondered where all the years had gone. She was now fifty-nine and her thoughts drifted to the past when she was only in her forties. She could not believe how time had slipped by so quickly, especially the last eight years.

Fiona loved to travel and had been lucky enough to get a job writing for a travel magazine after her divorce. Not only had she not had any time to be depressed about her failed marriage, but she had been given the chance to see the world while being paid to do it. Most of the time she cruised, which she loved, since touring the world while unpacking once held a lot of appeal to her.

Married not too long after college, she thought she would be wedded forever. Jason had seemed the perfect man for her and their first fifteen years together had been happy. The only factor that had marred her happiness was her husband's insistence they wait a few years to have children. By the time he agreed to try, for some reason Fiona had not been able to conceive. She had gone to the doctor and he had run tests and determined there was no reason for her not to get pregnant. When she asked Jason if he would go to the doctor for tests, he had refused. Fiona had no idea Jason had decided he never wanted to have children and had taken it upon himself to have a secret vasectomy early in their marriage. He knew by having the surgery his wife could never "accidentally" get pregnant. Meanwhile her doctor told her to relax and not worry about it. He thought if it was meant to be it would happen.

With the advent of computers and changing technology, Jason had lost his job. He realized he needed to go back to school to update his skills. Instead he became depressed about his changing life and began to drink. He floated from one mediocre job to another. Meanwhile Fiona took a job at a local newspaper doing a little bit of everything. It was at that time she discovered she had a talent for writing. She began honing her skills which would eventually lead to her travel writing position.

For twelve years she had battled with her husband's alcohol addiction. Many times he would quit, especially when some new drug came on the market that decreased his desire for drink. But inevitably he would fall off the wagon and it seemed as if each time he drank more than previously when he started again.

Jason was never a mean drunk. He just locked himself up in his home office at night and drank. Sometimes he would take off and Fiona would not see him for a week or more. This usually happened after he lost a job and had money to spend. At first she was worried about him but he was always spotted at some local tavern so she knew he was relatively safe. Whenever he did come home he would be very apologetic promising never to do it again. And, of course, she would believe him.

Fiona knew she was not fooling anyone, especially her mother, by trying to hide Jason's drinking. Her friends and family knew she was in denial and although she believed things would eventually get better, they never did.

One afternoon when he had been gone for several days, her friend Kathy had confronted her. "Fiona, when are you going to wake up and leave Jason? Don't you realize he has a girlfriend who drinks as much as he does? All you are doing is enabling him. You are too good of a person to put up with the kind of life you are living."

"Oh, Kathy! How do you know he has a girlfriend? Even though we have not had any relations for a few years, I never dreamed he might be seeing another woman."

"With his alcoholic condition, I doubt if they have any sex. I think it's a relationship based on companionship since they both have the drinking in common."

After being in denial for years, mortified by her husband's betrayal and knowing all her friends were talking about him, she was finally spurred to action. Realizing nothing would change she took the next morning off from work to see a divorce lawyer. The attorney strongly insisted she attend an AA support group meeting before starting any action against her husband. He had seen too many cases where he had begun divorce proceedings and then the addicted spouse had talked their partner out of continuing the action. Sometimes it would be years, if at all, before the divorce would happen.

Taking his advice, Fiona began going to a weekly support group. She discovered there were other people, both men and women, who were going through what she was. Learning that all she was doing was enabling her husband as Kathy had said, she knew she had to be strong and move on with her life. Three weeks later when Jason had once again been gone for several days, Fiona went back to the lawyer and began divorce proceedings.

That afternoon she had the locks on the doors of their home changed. Spending the evening packing up Jason's clothes, she stored the boxes in the unattached garage. It did not take the attorney long to find Jason's girlfriend's address and confirm he was staying there. Three days later her husband was served with divorce papers and told where he could claim his clothes.

Although he tried several times to contact her, she had steadfastly refused to speak to him and did not answer the door when he came to the house. She wanted nothing to change her resolve. Her AA support group mentor had warned her Jason would try and talk her out of divorcing him. But Fiona knew there was no way she would take him back. Previously she had always acceded to her husband's wishes. However once she made up her mind to do something it was very rare for her to change direction.

Jason finally confronted Fiona in the newspaper parking lot one afternoon. Realizing nothing would change her mind, he finally agreed to proceed quickly. He had already moved in permanently with his girlfriend, Vicky, and felt a lot better not having Fiona constantly harping on his drinking.

Since their incomes had never been very high, the only asset they had of any worth was their home. This factor, coupled with no children, kept the divorce very simple. Fiona decided she wanted the house, since it would help her net worth. She had been putting some money into a 401K at work and the newspaper had also contributed to the fund. With the backing from her investments she remortgaged her home.

Over the years they had built up a little equity in the house, so even her new mortgage payments were not much more than they had been paying. Some of that was due to the fact that mortgage rates had gone down quite a bit from when they originally bought the house. She wondered why they had never bothered to refinance with the lower rates. She realized Jason had always insisted on controlling their finances, and would have never listened to her advice.

She was able to pay Jason for his half of their home

which meant he no longer had any control over her emotionally, physically or financially. She knew he would probably drink his part of the money up in no time, but that no longer mattered to her. Her mother, Maggie, had wanted to loan her the money she needed; but Fiona refused. Actually she had felt empowered when she was able to refinance the house loan in her name alone.

"Mom, you know us O'Reilly's always need to be self sufficient. I love you dearly, but this is something I need to do for myself. I am just sad that after so many years of marriage we have so little to show for our time together."

Her mother had always been proud of her. They had always been close. When other mothers had trouble with their teenage daughters, Fiona had been a pleasure to be around. Maggie would offer advice but had never interfered with her daughter's decision making. She felt the only way Fiona would ever be a strong person was to take responsibility for her own actions. That was not to say, her mother had not offered guidance. But since their relationship had no control issues, the two women had formed a strong bond.

It was not long before Fiona and Jason were in the lawyer's office signing the final papers. Since she had started the divorce proceedings, she was the one who would have to go to court. As long as Jason signed the papers, as he was now doing, his presence in the courtroom was not required.

Fiona had wanted separate lawyers, but her husband had refused. Not wanting to waste money for two lawyers, Jason had insisted they use the same one. Fiona's attorney did not think it was a good idea. However with so few assets to divide, he had agreed. It was the first time they had been together since she had refused to talk to him in the newspaper parking lot.

ter, but only prolonging the little time she had left on earth, she had gone through the stages of grief rather quickly.

At first there had been denial and then anger that her condition had overtaken her. Finally she had tried bargaining with God. "If only she could have enough time left to know Fiona found happiness with someone…" And then the terrible depression hit and she could hardly get out of bed in the morning.

Maggie went through the last of the chemo treatments because Fiona had insisted. But, she was reaching acceptance of her fate and really did not want to go through with the radiation therapy. Maggie just wanted the agony of prolonging her life to end. Spending some quality time with her daughter was now what she looked forward to. In addition she did not want her brain all fuzzy from drugs before she had time to get all her affairs, including funeral arrangements, in order.

Fiona did not need to go on another trip for awhile since she had plenty of back articles she could write. All she wanted to do was spend as much precious time with her mother as possible. Her employer had no problem with her new schedule. Her pieces were well received whether about cruising or some other travel related subject. As long as she continued submitting articles to him, he was happy.

After lunch in the hospital cafeteria, and with a heavy heart, the afternoon passed and she was finally allowed to take her mother home. Maggie had been given several anti-nausea pills and she was sleepy from the medication. Tucking her mother into bed she sat holding her hand for about an hour.

By the time they had arrived home the earlier snow had already melted but Fiona knew it was too cold to sit on their balcony. Getting a glass of wine from the refrigerator she sat on the loveseat that overlooked the lake. She watched as the moon began to rise, casting a light on the water that seemed to create a path right to her balcony door. Sometimes when she stood in certain areas of her home and looked out at the lake, it almost seemed like she was standing on the balcony of her stateroom on some cruise ship looking out at the ocean.

Fiona and her mother had been so close over the years they could read each other's thoughts. The two of them had researched Maggie's disease together. They both knew the treatments and risks and the eventual outcome. This last chemo treatment had really taken a toll on Maggie. Fiona had a feeling her mother was going to refuse the radiation treatments. Many times when the person dying had reached acceptance, the family members were still stuck back in the denial phase. This was not the case with Fiona. She had gone through the stages of grief almost as quickly as Maggie, although she did not think she could ever reach acceptance.

Now all she wanted was what her mother wanted--meaningful time together before the end. She realized how lucky she was to have a job that would allow her to do that. She would work when her mother was sleeping and spend quality time with her when she was awake. Feeling a lot better after coming to terms with the reality of the situation, she was finally able to sleep soundly for the first time in weeks.

The condo's dining room had a balcony door that overlooked the lake and the next morning as they ate breakfast, her mother began talking about her treatments as she looked out at the water.

"Mom, I know what you are going to say. You do not want radiation. I will agree to anything you decide. I do not want to argue with you about anything. I just want our last days together to be as happy as possible."

the fall she wanted to be traveling again. By that time she knew she would be ready for new adventures.

Meanwhile she had decided to sell the condo. There were too many memories of her mother in the place and it was way too big for her now. Saying he would have no trouble selling her home, even though it would take a special buyer, a realtor friend placed it on the market. There were always people looking for her size condo on the lake. And the money she would make on the sale of her present condo would be quite substantial since she and her mother had lived there for three years and the building had sold out the first year.

Meanwhile she made an offer that was accepted on a two bedroom condo that had recently been put on the market in her building. She loved where she lived, but just did not need such a big home. A two bedroom condo would be perfect. There was enough room to put a sofa sleeper in the second bedroom for guests as well as her office furniture.

And so Fiona got on with her life. She spent a wonderful carefree summer with her friends. Kathy and Eric owned a cabin cruiser and they spent many fantastic weekends on the boat. Many of her cronies tried to fix her up with men they knew, from divorced to widowers. Some of them became companions on casual dates. But when they realized Fiona was not interested in them except as friends, they moved on.

Accepting her life as it was, she decided she loved her gypsy lifestyle. She still missed her mother and felt the ache in her heart every morning when she awoke. But not having a man in her life did not bother her at all. After the way Jason had deceived her, she did not know if she could ever trust a man again. She knew there were many good men around. Eric was a perfect example. But how do you go about finding someone trustworthy? She had trusted and believed in her husband and look where that had gotten her. No. She definitely was not interested in a relationship with any man. Not liking to dwell on anything negative for too long she let go of thoughts of some man changing her life.

identities of the others she would be working with. A couple of days later her travel arrangements arrived by email, as well as a list of who was on the panel.

Bryan McManus was bringing his wife Diana. Fiona did not know much about Bryan so she "Googled" him. Bryan was in his mid fifties and had built a respectable reputation as a travel writer. He and Diana had recently married, she for the first time, after spending years building their careers in the San Francisco area. Diana was about the same age as her husband, and worked at the same magazine as he did. She was a well known award winning photographer who had traveled the world on photo assignments. Obviously they had a lot in common. Fiona wondered what had brought them together.

This was quite a mix of people from the travel writing industry who would be on board ship with her. Finally, there was a man named Devlin O'Neill. She could not find out much about him. His biography said he was fifty-two and had been a Network and Telecommunications Manager before retiring two years ago. He had traveled all over the world for his job, so she guessed that qualified him for the work he did now. He worked for a magazine in Chicago, as did Fiona, so she concluded he probably lived somewhere around the Chicago area.

Fiona thought it was interesting that, of all the people invited, she and Devlin did not have traveling companions. Thinking out loud, Fiona realized Devlin was seven years younger than she was. I guess I do not have to worry about him coming on to me. Maybe we can become friends since it seems everyone else is matched up. But, in truth, Fiona was so used to traveling alone that if they did not pair up it would not bother her. She liked being on cruise ships as well as having a cabin to herself. And since you could be seated with others at meals, she always had companions to talk to while dining.

Chapter Four

It was 6:00 a.m. on a Friday when Fiona jumped out of bed as her alarm went off. Her suitcase and carry-on bag were packed by the door, as well as her computer which went everywhere she did. As she looked out the window, she saw that it was still dark; an indication that winter was not far off. Gone were the summer days when the sun rose early.

She had ordered Supershuttle to arrive at 6:45 a.m. since her flight was at 9:00 a.m. Milwaukee's airport was small enough that one-and a-half-hours before the flight was plenty of time to arrive. She had programmed her coffee pot to brew just before she awoke. Pouring herself a cup, she went into her bathroom to put on her make-up and got dressed. Fiona liked to shower in the evening since it saved her a lot of time on travel mornings. By 6:30 a.m. she was washing her coffee pot and cup and with a last look around, locked her door, and waited patiently for the elevator to come. She was headed for the indoor garage. There was a door there which led to the outside driveway where the van would pick her up.

She did not have long to wait. It was less than five minutes when she saw the blue colored van that would take her to the airport. Traffic was not too heavy and by the time she went through security and arrived at her gate it was 7:45 a.m. She still had a good hour before take-off, so she took out her computer to check for last minute instructions from her office.

Chapter Five

The next morning Fiona was awake by 7:00 a.m. She knew she could not board the cruise ship until noon. She had been able to turn in her rental car at the hotel the previous evening and had made a reservation for 11:00 a.m. to take the hotel shuttle to the port. So she had plenty of time to kill.

Not ready for breakfast, she decided to take a walk. She had just started out and had stopped to look at a shell when she saw a man walking behind her. Oh, no. It couldn't be, she was thinking!

As he passed by, not thinking what she was saying, she blurted out, "Why are you following me?"

When the man saw who it was, without saying a word, he turned around and started walking the beach in the opposite direction.

By the time Fiona got back to the hotel she realized she only had an hour before her shuttle. She knew she would get plenty of food on the ship, so she ordered toast and coffee from room service as she jumped into the shower. She had not felt too bad while out by the water since there had been a little breeze; but the Florida humidity had definitely wilted her. She was glad she had put on a sundress, instead of slacks, for her walk because it was now wet from sweat and pants would have been much too warm.

Putting on a pair of tan capris and a white short-sleeve blouse, Fiona found it was almost time to board the shuttle bus to the cruise terminal. As she walked to the lobby she spied the man sitting there next to the only empty chair in sight for the shuttle area. There was no way she was going to get away from him. With a sigh Fiona realized he was probably going on the same cruise as she was.

"Well, I guess there is no escaping it," she said as she sat down next to him. "Since ours is the only ship in port today, I guess you are going on the same cruise as me."

"Apparently so. Look I do not mean to be rude. I think we got off on the wrong foot yesterday. Thinking I would never see you again I just did not bother to talk to you after our altercation. My name is Devlin."

"Not Devlin O'Neill, the travel writer?"

As she watched the puzzled frown on Devlin's face, Fiona burst out laughing. "My name is Fiona Noonan."

"Oh, no! You're kidding? But why would you joke about that?"

"Do you think we could start over?" Fiona asked as she stretched her hand out to him.

"Absolutely," he said as he took her hand, shaking it in agreement.

"Who knows? Maybe someday we will become friends and laugh about how we met," Fiona said chuckling as she shook his hand.

"I certainly hope we will not become rivals like Brody and Peter. Although I hear they are pretty friendly when they are alone."

"What is your cabin number, Devlin?"

"I am on the Longitude Deck Eleven in 1122."

"I am on Deck 11, too. I am right next to you in 1120. I bet they put all of us together up there. The higher up top, the smoother the ride and it is obvious they want us curious. Why don't you have a companion?"

Fiona was thinking that could not be the whole story. Just because he had a failed marriage when he was young, did not mean he was supposed to spend his life as a celibate. She had the feeling there had been another woman in his life somewhere along the line. Although he had not said so, Fiona was correct in her assessment.

Shannon had been the love of Devlin's life. He had met her when he was thirty-six and they had spent six blissful years together. The only thing that had marred their relationship was Shannon's refusal to marry him. Then one morning Shannon had awakened with a terrible headache. Before the week was over she had been diagnosed with a brain tumor and the doctors insisted on immediate surgery. The rate of success for this type of surgery was very high, and so the two of them were very positive of the outcome being favorable.

Shannon had even agreed to marry Devlin as soon as she was feeling better. Then on the operating table, a blood clot had broken loose and Shannon was dead. Devlin could not believe that in less than a week the woman he loved was gone. Shannon had only been thirty-eight! It had taken Devlin many years to get over the pain of losing Shannon. Every once in a while he would still be overcome with grief, but the extreme pain had lessened over the years.

The reason Devlin had snapped at Fiona, and had never excused himself, was Fiona had the same hauntingly blue eyes as Shannon had. Seeing Fiona looking up at him from the boat had brought the pain back so swiftly that Devlin had lashed out at her. So Fiona was right. There was more to his story. Like her, Devlin had never wanted to have another serious relationship. Losing someone was just too painful, and he never wanted to experience that agony again.

Realizing it was her turn to answer his questions, Fiona looked at Devlin and said, "I have been divorced for quite a few years now and we never had any children."

Devlin noticed Fiona wince when she said she had no children and wondered what that was all about.

Fiona continued, "I am like you, Devlin. I have no intention of getting involved with anyone again. My mother just died recently or she would have come along with me. Having a daughter you are close to has to be wonderful. My mother and I were also extremely close. I live a little north of Milwaukee, Wisconsin, so we live a couple of hours from each other. Now I guess that is enough personal information from both of us. How about we study the ship's layout?"

Devlin could sense there was a lot more to her story than she had let on, but he assumed since they were only going to be friends, he should not press her for the details. He might have asked some more questions about her life if there had been a possibility of them dating. But since that was not going to happen, he let any other queries go. They had just begun forging a friendship after a very rocky start, which he knew was mostly his fault, so he did not want to get too personal.

As they picked up the brochures with the ship's information listed, two men interrupted them.

"Well, well, if it isn't Fiona Noonan. I recognize you from your picture. We "Googled" you so we would know something about you. Who is this man…your traveling companion?"

As she looked at the man speaking to her, Fiona recognized Brody Graham immediately. He was a short stocky man with a bald head. He wore heavy black framed glasses and a bowtie that were his trademark. She had gone to one of his seminars a few months previously, and had been in-

Chapter Six

It was not long before Fiona heard the signal on the loud speaker announcing the lifeboat drill. She had already taken her lifejacket out of the closet and placed it on a chair before she began unpacking.

Carrying her lifejacket, she exited her room. Several people were coming out into the hallway. She recognized Miriam and her mother as well as Peter and Brody. As she turned towards the stairs Devlin also came out of his room.

Everyone had to go to their muster stations which were arranged by location of the staterooms. Miriam and her mother, Emma, were loudly arguing and the crew in charge of their area had to silence them. Peter and Brody were standing to her left and Devlin to her right. Miriam and her mother were behind Peter and Brody and another couple was standing behind Fiona and Devlin.

Fiona looked behind her and saw a man about six feet tall with bright red curly hair. If he was Bryan he would be in his mid fifties, although both he and the woman next to him looked to be in their forties. The man was in terrific shape and Fiona knew he spent time in the gym. The woman was of medium height and only came up to his shoulder. She had short black hair cut in a pixie style and twinkly brown eyes Fiona noticed as the woman looked at her. She also was in good physical shape and they appeared a very compatible couple.

After instructions were given as to what to do in a real emergency and roll call taken, the passengers were dismissed. Miriam and Emma quickly left arguing once again while Peter and Brody hung back. Fiona turned to the man behind her and asked him if he was Bryan McManus. She had "Googled" the man but his picture had been very grainy, so it was hard to tell. In addition he was much younger looking than his actual age, if it was him.

"Yes, I am. And this is my wife, Diana."

"It's nice to meet the two of you," Fiona said and then introduced Devlin and Peter and Brody to the couple.

"Devlin and I are taking our life jackets back to our rooms and then going to the Lido deck for the 'sail away party'. Would you care to join us? And you, too, Peter and Brody?"

They quickly agreed to meet by the bar for the ship's sailing. Although they had all been on many cruises, they were supposed to be writing and critiquing life aboard a cruise ship. They felt they should experience as many activities offered on this new superliner as possible just as any of the other travelers would. They realized this was a job, not a vacation, even though they had been welcomed to bring a guest. The reason they had been invited on board was due to being the top people in their profession and they took their responsibilities seriously.

That did not mean they could not have fun. They met by the bar on the Lido deck but since the food, including the buffet, was located on this deck; it was extremely crowded. The band was playing calypso music and the cruise director was making several announcements about the evening festivities. Taking a glass of the free champagne, they walked one deck up to the Latitude deck.

Chapter Seven

Fiona had coffee delivered to her room at 7:00 a.m. She wanted to write some of her thoughts down about the ship before she met the others for breakfast. When she looked up from her computer she saw it was already 8:30 a.m. Nothing like being late for our first meeting she was thinking.

As Fiona entered the dining room everyone turned and looked at her.

"Sorry I am late everyone. I was working on my computer and time got away from me."

They all nodded at her, but the most surprising thing Fiona noted was Miriam sitting at the table sans momma.

"I guess since you are apologizing for being late, I will have to apologize twice for my behavior last night."

"There is no need to say anything, Miriam. I guess your mother is not coming to breakfast? I am glad someone told you we were meeting this morning."

"No one told me we were meeting. I just walked in and saw everyone. But then that is my fault after my rude behavior last night. And my mother is not a morning person. I am sure she will have some food delivered to her cabin when she wakes up. Besides we are supposed to be working, so my mother does not need to be here."

Fiona, along with the others, was surprised by Miriam's remarks. She almost appeared nice, which was something she was not known for.

Taking the lead, Brody said, "Well enough of all that. I am glad you found us Miriam. Since today is a day at sea we have a lot of things to cover. I have a suggestion. Since there are so many activities this morning why don't we divide up what is on the schedule. Between us we can cover everything that way. Then we can meet for lunch and see how the morning's activities went. If it is agreeable we will do the same thing after lunch. Then we can meet later this afternoon and discuss what we thought."

"Put me down for the wet T-shirt contest this afternoon."

Brody just rolled his eyes at Peter and tried to ignore his snickering.

Well it looks like the fun is about to begin Fiona thought. Peter and Brody may be partners in their private life but their public personas were always opposite. She also was wondering who made Brody chairman. Then she looked at Devlin and realized with a start he was thinking the same thing when he winked at her. She felt unnerved knowing his thoughts. She immediately picked up her pen while looking down at the pad of paper she had placed next to her plate.

Get a hold of yourself Fiona, she chided herself. He is just another writer here. And he is seven years younger and a more inexperienced travel writer. But she could still feel her cheeks redden with embarrassment. She could not help but be drawn to him. He was a very good looking man and very even-natured. Several times the previous night he had her in stitches with some of his comments, and she realized she could not help but like him.

Fiona knew she had come a long way from her initial impression of him. But since she had rarely dated, much less had a serious relationship, since her divorce; she had. Plus the aquarium in that famous hotel was awesome and she never grew tired of visiting it.

The excursions on Grand Bahama Island, where Freeport was located, were much easier to divide up because there was not as much going on there. Miriam and her mother would do the Island tour and shopping excursion. Fiona and Devlin would do the glass bottom boat as she had requested. Bryan and Diana would do a jeep tour of the island and then snorkel in the afternoon. That way they could compare the snorkeling on the two islands. That left Peter and Brody to do the Dolphin encounter.

All the writers were very pleased with the choices they had been given and were happy they all seemed to cooperate so well with each other. It was amazing how Miriam almost seemed a different person when her mother was not around.

Chapter Eight

The others quickly got up and left the table as soon as the assignments were sorted out. Still a little upset by Brody's take charge attitude, Fiona turned to Devlin and said, "I am really sorry to be putting you in this spot. It was not my intention to have you stuck with me for the whole cruise."

"Don't worry about it. We are really both to blame, if you want to call it blame, for not bringing a partner. I did not think it would be such a big issue. Since I am new at this profession, I just thought there would be some of us who came as singles. I saw Peter and Brody's names and assumed they were singles. As long as everyone else is paired up it is inevitable that we will be paired, since we are technically the only singles."

"I guess we will have to be resigned to that. All the same, I do not want you to think I don't like you or do not want to be with you. Actually I enjoy your company. Despite our rocky start we are pretty like-minded as to our work methods, and I think we can become friends. I just wanted to let you know I am not purposely trying to team up with you."

"Fiona, I realized that as soon as Brody took charge. And the same goes for me towards you. So now that we have cleared the air, I think your gem talk will be starting soon. I am off to the shore excursion talks. Since I have not

Chapter Nine

Usually the captain had a dress up cocktail party on the first day at sea but for some reason he had decided to hold it on their last sea day. So once again "resort casual" was the evening dress code. Fiona kept to her basic colors but this time reversed the order. Tonight she was wearing black slacks and a cream short sleeve sweater. She also put on her black sandals, a black pearl necklace and carried a small black handbag.

Fiona smiled when she saw Diana. Obviously the two women thought alike since Diana's outfit was very similar to hers. And, of course, the men once again had navy blue jackets on without ties. Last night both Bryan and Devlin had worn beige pants and tonight they both had white pants on.

Fiona was thinking that people who saw the two couples together might think they were related since their attire was so similar. They all arrived at the bar just before 7:00 p.m. and were able to order their Happy Hour wine.

Money was never used on a cruise ship. At the beginning of the cruise when you checked in, you gave the staff your credit card. After that all transactions were charged on your key card. On board ship it was a cash-less society, except in the casino, but sometimes that was a double-edged sword. Fiona imagined at the end of a cruise some passengers got "sticker shock" when they received their final bills. It was so easy. You charged your alcoholic drinks, shore excursions, shopping, photos and tips. If you were not careful, when the cruise was over you could owe more than you originally paid for your trip.

Devlin gave his key card to the waiter for their wine indicating he was paying for his and Fiona's.

"Devlin, I do not want you paying for my drinks."

"I have no intention of paying for all your drinks. I just thought it would be easier for me to pay tonight. I appreciated the extra tips you gave me on what to do this afternoon. So I thought I would go first. The next half priced Happy Hour can be your treat."

Fiona was still not very happy with the situation. She was used to paying her own way and did not want to start a sticky precedent. However, she realized this was not the time to start an argument. Besides she was worried they would have to deal with arguments soon enough when they went to dinner.

When their drinks were ordered, Bryan and Diana got up to dance. The music tended to be mellow and slow at this time of day.

"You know it is pretty obvious those two had a relaxing day. They both look like they got a little sun."

"They did spend a little time by the pool, but Bryan told me they never had a chance for a honeymoon. From the look of things I think they had a chance to spend some time in their cabin, too."

Fiona, a little embarrassed by the direction of the conversation, decided to change the subject and asked Devlin about his afternoon.

The two of them were so engrossed in their conversation they did not realize Bryan and Diana had spent almost a half an hour dancing. All of a sudden they heard Bryan say, "You better take your wine glasses with you. It is time to go to dinner."

They followed each other down the stairs to the dining room and were the first ones seated at their table. Before long Peter and Brody joined them. Both men appeared a little tipsy. Devlin had told Fiona that the art auction had included free champagne, and it was obvious Brody had been drinking for most of the afternoon.

On the way to her massage Fiona had passed Peter at the pool bar watching the wet T-shirt contest. It was easy to assume he had been imbibing most of the afternoon since he had a drink in front of him when she spotted him.

"Oh, look at you two. I guess all you men decided on a standard dress code."

As they looked at each other, everyone began laughing. All four of the men had navy blue jackets and white pants on. And none of them had a tie.

"Great minds think alike," Brody said to Fiona with a wink.

All of a sudden Fiona heard Diana gasp and Bryan groan. Turning to glance in the direction they were looking, Fiona saw two women walking very unsteadily towards them. It was Miriam and Emma! Obviously they had not missed their martini tasting.

Tonight Miriam had a long purple sheath with a purple feather boa around her neck. Naturally she was carrying a purple handbag and had a purple topaz necklace and earrings on.

Only Miriam can spend a lot of money on jewelry and still look tasteless Fiona thought. And, Emma! She had on another "prom dress." Last night's had been yellow, but tonight's was pink! And it was obvious she had several petticoats on underneath as had been the fashion in the 1950s.

There certainly was no accounting for taste when it

came to those two women. And, as on the previous night, they were arguing all the way to the table.

None of the others could figure out why Miriam brought her mother along on her trips. She was a totally different person when she was away from Emma. And why subject yourself to the emotional abuse that spewed from the woman's mouth if you did not have to? It was clearly a mystery.

The two women kept at it throughout most of the dinner. Even the waiters stayed away from their table unless absolutely necessary. Everyone was uncomfortable and just wanted dinner to be over as quickly as possible. Luckily they had the show to go to at 10:00 p.m., and somehow they made it through dinner.

Finally before the desserts were served, Brody had enough.

"Miriam, you and your mother will not be welcomed at this table anymore unless you can be quiet and stop arguing. Maybe you do not care about ruining your dinner, but we were all looking forward to a leisurely meal. You two have totally spoiled our entire dining experience."

At that Emma got up to leave and fell flat on her face. Drinking wine throughout her dinner had probably not helped to steady her. Miriam, giving Brody a nasty look, picked up her mother and practically dragged her out of the dining room.

At first the table was extremely quiet. But after the waiter had taken the dessert orders, Bryan turned to Brody and said, "On behalf of my wife and I, thank you, Brody."

As the man looked around the table he saw Fiona, Devlin and Peter nodding in agreement. That was just what they all needed to break the ice. Soon they were all laughing and enjoying each other's company. When they finished the dessert, the six of them went to the showroom together.

Tonight's show was a comedian, and that was Fiona's least favorite type of show. As she looked around the theater, Fiona could not see Miriam anywhere. So much for attending to duty. Taking care of her alcoholic mother must be more important Fiona thought.

As soon as the show was over Devlin suggested a nightcap in the piano bar. Since Fiona loved piano bars, she quickly agreed to go with him. The other four all wanted to go to their rooms since they were getting up early for their Nassau excursions in the morning.

Devlin and Fiona walked up the stairs to the piano bar. This time they each paid for their own drinks. At least, since it appeared the two of them would be paired up most of the cruise, they were very companionable. But Fiona did not really care if Devlin had escorted her or not. She loved piano bars and she always felt very comfortable going on her own when she was on a ship. She probably would have come up for a nightcap after the show on her own if he had not suggested it.

After about an hour they agreed they had had a big day, and since tomorrow would be even busier, they were soon saying goodnight at their cabin doors.

As Fiona entered her stateroom she was thinking about how she had been alone, except for her mother, for such a long time. Even though she was used to it, she had forgotten how much fun it could be to have someone to talk to or just to have as a companion. She enjoyed Devlin's friendship but doubted they would see each other after the cruise was over. But, at least, they could enjoy each other's company for these next few days.

Chapter Ten

What a beautiful day in paradise! Fiona's alarm went off a little after 6:00 a.m. A few minutes later she heard a knock on her door. She knew the room service waiter had arrived with the coffee she had ordered before going to bed.

She had the waiter put the tray on the table out on her balcony. Taking a cup in hand she sat in a chair and watched the scene unfolding before her. The cruise ship was in the process of docking, and the city of Nassau and Paradise Island beckoned her. Of all the places she visited on her travels, this was definitely one of her favorites. And also one she never grew tired of coming back to.

The temperature was already in the low seventies. In the summer the weather was stifling and humid but from fall through spring the temperatures were usually in the high seventies with lower humidity. She spied the pink and white Parliament building as she sipped her coffee.

Downtown Nassau was always so colorful with the buildings painted yellow, pink, coral, teal and so many other rainbow colors. And Fiona remembered there was quite a history associated with New Providence Island.

Christopher Columbus had landed on the island in 1492, but only discovered a few Indians living there. The Spaniards followed but left very quickly when they found no gold. So the city was not founded until 1650 by the British who called it Charles Town. Not long after that the waters surrounding the town became dominated by pirates including Blackbeard. The Spanish government became infuriated when the British refused to help stop the pirates, so they burned Charles Town to the ground. A year later in 1695, the town was rebuilt and named Nassau.

Nassau had its up and downs over the next two hundred years. It was not until prohibition that the island really began to prosper. Resorts were built and in 1929 the first casino opened. When that happened Pan Am brought wealthy American tourists from Miami on the short forty-five minute plane ride to drink and gamble. The gambling, along with the opening of many prominent banking facilities, led to the economic development Nassau needed to thrive. The area had also become well-known when many of the James Bond stories were filmed there. The Bahamians, as they are known, were prohibited from gambling. This resulted in a lack of crime usually associated with gaming towns. Fiona could not believe it when she looked at her watch. She had been sitting on her balcony musing about the city and the many sites around the ship for almost an hour. It was just about 7:30 a. m. and she had told Devlin she would meet him at 8:00 a.m. for breakfast.

Dressing in a pair of white capris and a pink T-shirt, she looked as colorful as the city around her. It was not long before she was off to meet Devlin for one of her favorite activities on board ship, breakfast by the pool. Although the regular buffet was inside in a large room, the pool area always had omelets, pancakes, waffles, and fruit stations set up. Everything you needed for breakfast could be found outside as well as inside. And she always enjoyed sitting and watching the bustling activities around the port while she ate.

Immediately spotting Devlin, who was already seated at a table with a cup of coffee, she walked out on deck. She could tell he was watching for her. Devlin knew he should not have romantic feelings towards her, but she seemed to stir his blood as she walked towards him. Feeling a little embarrassed and trying to hide his feelings behind his sunglasses, he inadvertently said, "You look very pretty this morning, Fiona." Then quickly realizing his slip-up, he said, "What I meant is you look very colorful. Pink certainly becomes you."

Fiona knew she was blushing from his compliment. Trying to hide her reaction she said, "Let's go get our breakfast and I can brief you on what to expect today."

Nodding his head Devlin joined her in the line to order omelets. By the time they got back to the table with their food, the moment was over and they seemed back to normal.

Fiona had not really taken Devlin's comment too seriously. After being married to her ex for so long and not having had marital relations much less compliments in years, she did not realize that a male might look at her in a romantic way. She was really oblivious to the fact that any man might be interested in her sexually. In addition, she was reaching the end of her fifties and Devlin had just entered his. The fact that he might be attracted to her in any way, besides as a friend, was totally incomprehensible to her.

As they were eating, Devlin noted what a small town atmosphere Nassau seemed to have.

"It's a pretty big island. I think the population is around two hundred thousand which is a lot since all of the Bahamas only has three hundred thousand. I know I read somewhere that seventy percent of the Bahamian population lives on this island. It really makes me wonder about Freeport, the other port we are going to. I love to visit Nassau but I have never been to Freeport. I am curious to ing for the moment. Let's go get our things and get in line for our first excursion. We can deal with what happens tonight when it happens."

Chapter Eleven

The two of them had a busy but fun day. Fiona was worried she would be bored with all the "touristy" things they were doing, but discovered she was having fun just being with Devlin. Everything was new to him, and she took delight in the simple pleasure he was having seeing everything for the first time. Since she loved Nassau, she was always happy to be around someone who felt like she did. And she could tell he was falling under the spell the island seemed to create.

They returned to the ship for a quick lunch before the afternoon trip to Atlantis. They had spent a little time downtown after the city tour at the straw market. There was no need to take a jitney out to Cable Beach because the city tour had included a drive there, so Fiona did not mind spending a little time downtown shopping.

Devlin told her he always liked to bring a little something back for his daughter. All the years he had been away for his previous job he had always brought her something back on his return. Even though she was now an adult, old habits die hard. He found a straw purse he thought she would like and a flowery island shirt for himself. He planned to wear his shirt with some white pants for dinner.

Fiona did not usually shop, but a long straight flowery dress that you slipped on caught her eye. While Devlin was buying his things, Fiona had gone off in a different by 4:00 p.m. so we had time to rest and relax before the evening."

Fiona noticed that the two men did not seem as tipsy as the night before. She figured they probably did not have as much to drink today. Just then the wine steward came over carrying a bottle of wine. Fiona was not really interested in more wine, but the bottle they were told was compliments of the captain and eight glasses were poured around the table.

"What about Miriam and her mother? Anyone see them today?" Devlin asked as the wine glasses were filled.

"We did see them and it was not a good situation," Brody answered

"What happened?" All four heads turned towards Brody as he continued.

"Miriam and Emma got back about the same time our excursion returned. It was obvious the two of them had been drinking, but Emma was especially intoxicated. She kept yelling at Miriam and her language was extremely colorful to say the least. Miriam was obviously trying to ignore her mother until Emma fell down flat on the gang-plank. Some of the ship personnel helped her up, and Miriam dragged Emma into an elevator. We were behind them, and that was all we could see."

"Sometimes I almost feel sorry for Miriam," Fiona said. "I don't know why she lets her mother emotionally abuse her like that. And it is so embarrassing not only for her but for everyone else around. You would think she would insist her mother stay home if she cannot act with decency."

Looking around the table Diana spoke. "I have known people who have been emotionally and verbally abused. It is not often easy for the abused person to break out of that pattern. Usually they are so beaten down or believe they are at fault, they cannot act with any decisiveness against the abuser."

"You are right, Diana," Peter added. "There is a rumor that has been going around the industry for years that Miriam was once secretly married but her mother broke it up when she found out."

"It would be so tragic if that story is true. I am surprised that Miriam did not go completely over the edge if that really happened. She is a very good writer. I know Bryan admires her work."

"Speak of the devil, so to speak," Peter said. All eyes turned towards the entrance as Miriam walked in without her mother. For a change she was not as outlandishly dressed as she had been the previous days. She had an island dress on but it was a plain long straight slip-over black dress. It was made of the cotton material that island dresses were made from and looked very simple, but almost stunning on Miriam in its simplicity. She was wearing black sandals and no jewelry except a gold cross around her neck.

"You look so nice tonight. What a pretty necklace, Miriam. Is your mother coming to dinner?"

"Mother was not feeling well this evening, Fiona, and decided to stay in our cabin. She said she would order room service if she gets hungry. As for the dress I don't know where it came from but I like it. And the necklace was given to me by someone special a long time ago," she said almost wistfully. "Where did the glass of wine come from?"

Peter explained about the captain's complimentary bottle. Everyone watched as Miriam moved her mother's glass next to her own.

"Shouldn't waste it," she smiled at the group.

At that point the waiter came over to take orders so

room. They saw Miriam leaving for dinner, but no one else went in or out of the cabin until Miriam was seen returning after dinner. At that point they knew Emma had not left the cabin by the door. Since it was standard procedure, a search of the ship was still being carried out. But they were doubtful of finding Emma anywhere on the ship.

Then the cameras positioned on the outside by their balconies were rewound. The pictures were very grainy and things were not very clear, especially since it was dark. However, three minutes before Miriam left for dinner some kind of dark object had fallen from their balcony. But the cameras did not show a second person and there was no proof that could hold up in any court that Miriam might have been involved or exactly what it was that did go overboard.

The ship had already turned around. As soon as they knew what time the situation had probably occurred, the computer immediately was able to calculate the return course. Once they arrived in the area the ship made circles for about an hour but there was no trace of anyone. Even if Emma could stay afloat hypothermia would have gotten her after about twenty minutes, and she would have drowned.

Finally they heard more bells and the ship started heading back towards Freeport again.

The First Officer had left during the search mission but had returned shortly after the last set of bells had rung.

"I am sorry Ms. Decker, we saw nothing out there. We might have kept searching but the Captain decided we needed to continue to Freeport so we are not too late arriving in the morning. It is important to stay on schedule as much as possible and since your mother disappeared awhile ago, it is doubtful she could have survived in the water much more than a half hour. The Captain did inform the home office and has written up a report. The authorities have also been notified in Freeport, and there will be representatives to meet us when we dock there tomorrow morning."

"I can stay the night with Miriam," Fiona volunteered.

"That is not necessary. I appreciate the offer but I think I am all cried out for the present. I just feel numb. My only prayer is if mother did fall overboard, she did not suffer much before the end. Maybe she fell down somewhere on the ship and is unconscious and we will still find her in the morning."

"That is very improbable, Ms. Decker. When we started looking for your mother at sea, we were methodically searched the ship at the same time. I do not want you to have any false hope. It is extremely unlikely your mother is on this ship unless she is in someone else's bedroom. Does she know any other passengers on board?"

"No, Sir, she does not. The only other people she knows on board besides the ones here with me now are two other travel writers, Peter Morrison and Brody Graham. They were in the dining room when I arrived tonight and are in the piano bar now. So I guess there is not much chance of finding her then?"

"It seems rather doubtful. Would you like me to send a woman crew member to sit with you in here tonight?"

"No. Thank you for your kindness. I just want to be alone right now. Don't worry. I will be fine."

The Captain had told the First Officer not to say anything to Miriam or the others about what they had seen on the cameras. If she had been involved with her mother going overboard that would be murder, and they did not want her to have a chance to come up with any explana-

"Did you schedule your shore excursion a little later today, too?"

"Yes, like you and Devlin, since we are doing the dolphin encounter, we thought the weather would be warmer if we waited to go a little later instead of going as soon as we docked."

Asking a waiter walking by for a cup of coffee Fiona added, "I have to tell you, Peter and Brody, I have never been to Freeport. I have always loved Nassau and was looking forward to coming here to compare the two places. But what I have seen so far is very disappointing."

"Brody, let me tell the two of them about this island."

Fiona watched as Brody nodded at Peter. That was another interesting situation for Fiona to consider. The two men were supposedly rivals but it was obvious Peter deferred to Brody."

Puffing up with obvious importance Peter started explaining. "This piece of land is called Grand Bahama Island. It has no early history as Nassau does. In 1955, Wallace Groves from Virginia had lumbering interests here and the Bahamian government granted him fifty thousand acres of swamp and scrubland. And that became the city of Freeport, so called because it is a free trade zone. The government agreed that businesses in Freeport would pay no taxes before 2054, and this created some terrific duty free shopping. What you are looking at here is the port, so it is not pretty and does not have the charm of Nassau."

"So is this all there is?"

"No, Devlin. This is the second largest city in the Bahamas. Naturally Nassau is first, but over seventy five thousand people live on this island. And over a million visitors a year make tourism the second biggest boom to their economy. We are only fifty miles from Palm Beach,

Florida, and there are thousands of flights here every year. Most of the tourists go to the little seaside suburb of Lucaya which is about eleven miles from the ship. There are hotels, golf courses, beautiful beaches, and of course, a casino in the village. You will see it today when you go on your shore excursion. They always stop at the Marketplace over there for some shopping time before returning to the ship."

Fiona groaned, "Just what I need more shopping!"

"Well it is nowhere on the scale of Nassau." It really feels more like a sleepy little beach town. But when the sun sets, the place comes alive with all the nightclubs and local bands entertaining the visitors. We will have sailed by then, so you will not get to experience that."

"To be truthful I prefer the piano bar at night, Peter. Now if you are finished telling us about Freeport, would you all like to hear a little gossip?"

All three men leaned forward looking at Fiona in anticipation while nodding their heads.

She told them about Miriam not answering her phone and then seeing her leave the ship with the officials. She also related the conversation she had with Ramon about Miriam and her mother's clothing.

"Well, getting rid of those clothes especially Emma's dresses, is no loss. I have friends who would not be caught dead in those outfits," Peter said, and then started blushing realizing he was talking about his sexual lifestyle.

Ignoring his comments while secretly agreeing with him, Fiona continued, "I just think it is a strange thing to do when Miriam does not know for sure her mother is dead. If she did not like her own clothes, why did she have to wait until her mother was not around to get rid of them? It is almost as if she knows she will never see her mother again."

"She did have all night to think about it, Fiona.

The ship has been checked from top to bottom including every stateroom this morning. Emma is nowhere on this ship. The obvious thing is she accidentally fell overboard last night. And I hate to say this but if some shark got her, there will never be any evidence found."

"You are right, of course, Devlin."

"Besides, Fiona, remember what Diana said about being emotionally abused? Maybe Miriam had an epiphany last night and realizing she is finally free of her mother's cruelty, she wanted to get rid of any reminder of her. I know she was crying a lot last night but that could have been shock. I know it sounds terrible, but now that she has had time to come to terms with the situation, she might feel carefree and happy for the first time in her life. Personally I think it was terrible the awful things that woman used to say to Miriam."

"There is a lot to be said about what you are saying, Devlin. Look how simple but nicely dressed Miriam looked last night when she knew her mother would not be with her. But I am surprised she would even have brought a dress like that with her on this cruise, since her mother would supposedly be with her every night."

"Maybe her mother gets sick from all her boozing at least one night whenever she is cruising with Miriam so she always brings one nice outfit. But who knows. Enough of all this talk of Miriam and her clothes," Brody said as he started getting up from the table. "As much as I love to gossip we only have twenty minutes to get down to the buses for our shore excursions. We can talk more about this tonight at dinner. I am sure Bryan and Diana will want to hear all the news.

Deciding they had chatted enough about the situation for the present, the four of them quickly ascended the two flights of stairs to their cabins to take care of some last minute things before leaving the ship.

Chapter Thirteen

The four writers met once again as they were leaving their staterooms. They took the elevator down to where the gangplank was located. Putting their keycards in the gangway machine so the crew would know they were no longer on board, they declined having their pictures taken by the ship's photographers as they disembarked. Crew members were quickly directing everyone to the proper lines for their shore excursions.

Peter and Brody turned and waved as they climbed on their bus for the dolphin encounter. As Fiona and Devlin boarded their bus they noticed all the front seats were taken so they moved to the back to be seated. The buses were older tour models and Fiona knew from her earlier research that they had previously had three or four owners before being brought to the islands. Since they no longer were needed for long distance travel, they were perfect for ferrying tourists around on shore excursions on islands.

Although Fiona offered the window seat to Devlin, he declined.

"These seats are pretty tight, Fiona. I prefer to sit by the aisle so I can stretch my legs out."

"It certainly does not look like you will miss much not sitting by the window." Fiona still was not very excited by what she saw of Freeport.

As Devlin smiled at her she felt her stomach do a

flip flop. Wow, what is that about she wondered? Feeling the side of his body pressed against her did not help the situation either. I have felt very compatible with Devlin and because of our age difference I have not really felt a sexual attraction to him. Why now?

Fiona remembered an article she read about death after her mother had passed away. It said that sometimes people yearned for a sexual outlet after someone they knew had died. It was an affirmation that the person still alive was able to feel and had the desire to continue living.

Maybe I just want to feel alive she assumed after deciding the worst had happened to Emma. For whatever reason, he fascinates me. Although friendly and talkative, he never reveals anything of himself. Maybe that is also why I am so interested in him. However, I was introduced to quite a few men last summer on Kathy's boat and I never obsessed about any of them like I am doing with him. I did not even like him when we first met. I have to get over this. I am not some teenager with a crush on some boy she knows. Actually I feel pretty foolish even feeling this way. I am sure he does not feel anything for me.

But Fiona was wrong about that. Devlin, too, was feeling drawn to her. He did not care about their ages, which was irrelevant as far as he was concerned. They were both mature adults who had a good time when together. He had not laughed with a woman, as he and Fiona were doing, since Shannon had died. He felt a little bittersweet remembering back to his life with Shannon. He was older now, and he knew he had changed. While Shannon would always be that same sweet thirty-eight year old who never aged.

He remembered some of the platitudes his friend Roy had said to him one night when they were out drinking about a year after Shannon's death. Roy had suffered through a terrible first marriage and finally divorced. Then out of the blue about three years after his divorce, he had fallen in love at first sight. Angela was so perfect for Roy, and Devlin knew they would be together the rest of their lives.

"You can't go forward in life, Devlin, until you let go of your heartache. You need to seize opportunities. Unexpected adventure can occur with the right woman. I know you do not want to think it is true right now but someday it will come about when you least expect it. Everything happens for a reason when the time is right. Your journey through life will be more enjoyable if you give yourself a chance to love again. It is definitely better to risk failure than to never know if you would have succeeded in finding someone to love."

Devlin was not ready to listen to Roy but he had stored the conversation in the back of his mind for future consideration.

"Don't frown like that, Devlin. You never know who is falling in love with your smile. I know a person can get hurt loving as deeply and passionately as you did, but it is the only way to live life completely. Don't think about tomorrow. Live each day as best you can. And when the time is right, and trust me it will happen, be open to new beginnings. Do not let the past hold you back."

Devlin wondered why he was remembering Roy's conversation now. Maybe Emma's probable death was making him relive Shannon's dying. The odd thing was it did not hurt as much now. I hate to say it, but time does seem to heal the pain. I still feel the ache that Shannon is gone but it is not as intense. I know I am still alive and I have to move on. I always thought Roy was rambling that night because he was so in love. But maybe he understood something I could not at that time.

I don't know why, but Fiona appeals to me. I have had plenty of time to meet other women. I do not know why her and why now. She makes me laugh, and we always have so much to talk about. It seems as though the more I am around her, the more she makes me feel. I wonder what she would think if she knew what I was thinking.

Not realizing what Devlin was musing about, Fiona knew she had to let go of her thoughts about him. She decided to listen to the tour guide talking about the island. She continued to watch out the window as she listened to the same history of the island Peter had told them earlier that morning. They passed some housing subdivisions but the island still did not have the charm of Nassau. They finally arrived in Lucaya but all Fiona saw were some high-rise condos and hotels and a large marketplace.

The guide reiterated that they would have some shopping time after their glass bottom boat adventure but that still did not excite Fiona. The whole area looked a little like the Cable Beach area in Nassau. It was pretty but Fiona knew she had no desire to ever return here.

As they neared the water the waves were rolling in, and this Fiona found way more appealing. The boat looked like a catamaran with seats and a cover overhead. As they boarded she noticed a large open area in the center of the boat. As she looked over the railing the bottom of the boat was covered in glass and she could see all the way to the ocean floor below. However, there was not a lot to see except sand, since they were so close to shore. The boat held forty people and everyone could stand in a square around the center and see the ocean bottom. There were seats by the outside railing so the passengers could sit if they got tired of standing.

The water was a beautiful aquamarine color that Fiona never grew tired of viewing. As soon as everyone boarded the captain got on the loudspeaker to welcome them and explain the few safety rules. Although they were welcome to look through the glass, the crew told everyone there would not be much to see until they navigated around to the east side of the island.

Fiona and Devlin sat on the benches and watched the water. Devlin spotted some dolphins and everyone looked in the direction he pointed. It was a very relaxing ride and with the cover overhead the sun was not too hot. The temperature had warmed up a few degrees from early morning and she was glad they had decided to take the later excursion.

The captain then announced that because the temperature had warmed up, they had been fortunate enough to see the dolphins. Usually they did not come around to this area until later in the day. As soon as they rounded the tip of the island the boat slowed down. Although the depth of the water could drop dramatically to a thousand feet in this area, there was a large reef averaging three to twelve feet with wonderful views.

Everyone found a place around the center railing. The sight was amazing. Fiona saw sea grass and many colorful fish. Plus the ocean bottom rose and fell more spectacularly here. In Nassau the boats just went back and forth in the bay by the cruise ships so although the water was clear, the view was not very dramatic. She was glad she had chosen to do this excursion here in Freeport. Fiona had never been crazy about snorkeling. A glass bottom boat had all the advantages of snorkeling without getting wet.

As she leaned over to get a better view she felt Devlin pressing against her side. She knew he could not help it since everyone was crowded into this small area, but she felt a flash of excitement run through her when the boat

Chapter Fourteen

Fiona was not really tired. When she returned to her cabin she took a shower since she was sweaty and dusty after her day out exploring the island. As she lay on her bed she started thinking about Bryan and Diana. They were so happy and seemed so in love. They acted like a young honeymoon couple even though they were in their mid fifties.

Being so in love at their age surprised her but then she started chiding herself. She was reasoning like a thirty year old. Just because they were both in their fifties did not mean they were dead sexually. Actually it made her feel good to realize that a couple could have a warm physical relationship no matter how old they were. It would not be long before she hit sixty. Having someone to trust and confide in might be nice. She knew she had a bad experience with her ex and decided maybe she should be more open to meeting someone.

Devlin was nice and they had a lot in common; but she felt he was far too young for her. She could hear her friends at home calling her a "cougar," and that did not please her. But maybe there was someone else out there she could fall in love with. It had happened for Bryan and Diana and maybe it could happen to her.

Bryan had told Devlin his story. Devlin in turn had confidentially told Fiona. Bryan thought he had been happily married for twenty-seven years. He had fallen in love and married a girl he had met in college when he was twenty-four. Then one day he had come home and was confronted by his wife. She wanted a divorce! She had reconnected on the internet with her high school sweetheart and had been secretly meeting him for months. She no longer wanted to live with the deception and wanted to move in with her boyfriend.

They had two children who were out of college and were making their own way in the world. Now it was her turn. She wanted to spend the rest of her life living as she pleased. Bryan could not believe his whole world was turning upside down. They had been saving money for their retirement and now everything they owned would be divided between them. He was powerless to change his wife's mind and within a couple of months he was without a wife or home. His world had totally changed.

His children could not believe what their mother had done. But the problem was they were leading their own lives and were too busy to realize how alone their father felt. So Bryan threw himself into his work. He traveled far and wide and not owning a home anymore soon ceased to bother him. He knew he would never trust another woman again.

Then as he neared almost ten years as a single man a miracle happened. Bryan had always known Diana casually, but not in a personal way. A few months previously they happened to find themselves together in the Middle East when rioting broke out. All the media were taken to a local hotel and told not to leave until the unrest was over. Bryan found himself eating his meals with Diana. Being fascinated with her work he started to get to know her. Because they were in such a volatile situation the two of them had started confiding in each other about their lives.

Bryan could not believe Diana had never had a serious relationship. And she ached for what his ex wife had joining them. They all agreed that it was a lot more enjoyable having dinner without a couple of drunk women at each other's throats.

After dinner they went to the show, and it was terrific. Having entertainment every night on board ship was a real plus when cruising. When the show was over, they all went for a nightcap in the piano bar. Considering what a diverse group they were Fiona marveled at how well they all got on together. She did wonder at one point how Miriam was faring. She would have been shocked to know that Miriam was living it up with a young male escort she had picked up while enjoying the famous Miami Beach night scene.

As for Devlin the evening was a very pleasant one. He sat next to Fiona during the show but found himself seated between Peter and Brody when they went to the piano bar. This was really for the best. He did not want Fiona to think he was avoiding her, but sitting between the two men took the pressure off of him to pretend he was not feeling anything sexual towards her.

In a way he did not want his time with her to end, but at the same time he was ready to go home. He was sure once he got away from Fiona these new sexual feelings coursing through him would fade away. He had no idea Fiona was thinking the same thing.

Since they had all taken naps that afternoon and tomorrow was a day at sea with no real reason to get up early, the six of them closed the piano bar down that evening. They knew they were meeting in the morning, but at the last minute Brody asked if a 10:00 a.m. breakfast meeting on the pool deck would not be more relaxing. They all agreed with him and decided to sit and eat their breakfast back in the hamburger and hot dog area. That is where they had found each other lunching this afternoon after their shore excursions. Since food would not be served in that area until at least 11:00 a.m. that would give them an outside area to converse with each other without a lot of people around.

After the piano bar closed they all went back to their staterooms. Waving good night to each other in the hallway, they entered their cabins.

she and Devlin had shared. She had also enjoyed having a glass of wine with Bryan and Diana every night. It was amazing how easily one slipped into a routine on board ship. Even going to the piano bar and having an after dinner drink would not seem the same without Peter and Brody pontificating on so many subjects.

As much as she enjoyed cruising Fiona was worried the next one would seem a little lonely without the others she now counted as friends. Maybe someday they would all be lucky to meet up again on another assignment.

Fiona had definitely had some negative impressions especially about Peter and Brody before the cruise, and it was wonderful how they had all gelled, after Miriam's mother's accident. It just goes to show you that people tend to bond more in times of stress or trouble; she was thinking.

Chapter Sixteen

At Devlin's knock she opened the door and saw Brody and Peter standing there, too.

"Wow! I guess I am being escorted by three very good looking men tonight."

Even though Peter and Brody could not be considered eligible all three men looked pleased she was glad to be with them.

"We ran into each other coming out of our cabins and decided it would be fun for you to walk into the bar with all three of us," Peter said with a great big smile.

"And Devlin has a story for you. But let's wait until we meet up with the others," Brody said.

You have no idea how much my story has changed from what you know Devlin was thinking to himself.

"I have to tell all of you, I was thinking about this cruise before you knocked on my door. I don't know if I will ever see any of you again, but I know I will miss all three of you. We have had such a fun time being together and have been very compatible considering we did not know each other previously and come from different walks of life."

Smiling at her words the four of them walked to Happy Hour thinking that Fiona had voiced exactly what they also felt about each other. Peter and Brody walked on either side of Fiona with Devlin behind her as they entered the bar. They knew they were going to meet Bryan and Diana, so Fiona scanned the area for the twosome. Spotting the couple Fiona started walking towards Diana who was waving from a table with four empty chairs.

All six of them were a little sad when they sat down. They all mentioned how much they had enjoyed each other's company and hoped they would meet again sometime.

Diana immediately asked Devlin if he had told Fiona about his big win. But, before he could say anything, the waiter came for their drink orders. After the waiter left to get their drinks Brody started telling everyone about the champagne auction that afternoon.

"First of all Bryan and Diana had never been to an art auction and wandered in towards the end. As they were drinking champagne Diana got totally caught up in the bidding. When a Thomas Kincaid print came up for auction she decided it was perfect for their new home and after several bids, much to Bryan's surprise, he discovered they now owned the print.

"I just love that print," Diana gushed. "I don't particularly like the mat or frame but I can have it changed when we get home."

"Anything for you, love," Bryan said as he looked at the others with a twinkle in his eyes.

"You already know, Fiona, about the contest the ship runs throughout the cruise called 'guess the price of the Picasso.' I think we all put in bids on the second day.

Just before the announcement telling someone had won Peter went to get Devlin who was playing charades in a small room on the same deck as the auction. He told us he was not interested in buying any art but wanted to see how they ran the auction and contest. So Peter promised to let him know when that part of the program was happening."

While nodding at Brody, Fiona said, "I forgot all about the contest. I ran into some people from Wisconsin and got so caught up in their life history that I never gave the auction a thought."

"Well," Brody continued, "as everyone sat waiting the auctioneer came on the microphone and said, 'I have to tell you I have been doing this job for five years and in all that time only one person has ever guessed the right amount. Today I have a second person who has correctly guessed the price of the Picasso. That price is sixty three thousand five hundred dollars.' At that point we all groaned because we knew we had not won."

Peter interrupted, "Devlin did not groan. He could not remember what he had guessed. We all looked around the room waiting for the lucky person to stand up. No one did. Then the announcer said, 'The winning entry is from Devlin O'Neill.' At that point Brody and I stood up and clapped Devlin on the back. Diana and Bryan also stood and started to shake his hand. Devlin just sat there with his mouth opened wide."

"I have never won anything before," he told the group.

Brody continued, "Devlin appeared totally shocked. Then I heard the auctioneer announce to the room that even though no one had stood up, he knew the winner was over on his left side since there was a circle of people surrounding a man and congratulating him. He then asked Devlin to go over to his assistant so they could verify who he was."

"Let me jump in now, Brody, because there is a lot more to this story that you are not aware of. Anyway the first thing I said was, 'Do you have to pay taxes on a win like this, Brody?' He answered 'No, Devlin, not when it is an art item. Why don't you go over to that woman and show her your key card, so they can identify you? Winning is really great, but it is almost as much fun knowing the winner. I bet Fiona will be surprised, too,' and I agreed."

As he continued he said, "I almost forgot about you, Fiona. I remembered it was you who insisted I put in a bid since you knew I was coming to check out the art auction this afternoon. I told the others that I wrote down your suggestion for the worth of the print. I really felt you were the one who should have won the Picasso. Then Brody asked if I wanted someone to go with me over to the auctioneer's assistant, but I said 'No,' I would be fine. I knew I was still somewhat in shock but that would pass very quickly."

As everyone looked at him Brody said, "What do you mean by that, Devlin?"

"At that point all the people were leaving the art area, and I said good-bye to all of you and walked over to the art assistant. I was thinking to myself; what am I going to do with a sixty three thousand dollar Picasso print? It really does not go with my home which is decorated with a nautical theme. And then I decided I would sell it and give half the money to you, Fiona. These and other thoughts were running through my head as I reached the assistant."

Laughing he continued, "I told the woman I was so surprised. I had never won anything before and the print was worth so much money. Then I heard the assistant say, 'You did not think you won the Picasso print, did you?' At this point I was utterly deflated and I said, 'I didn't win the print?' The poster said 'Guess the price of the Picasso print and win.' I assumed I won. But now you are telling me I did not win the Picasso?"

"Heaven's no, she laughed at me. Didn't you read the fine print? What you won are five prints by famous European artists. They are worth a couple of hundred dollars each."

"What?" Brody stared at him. "You didn't win the Picasso? That is an utter rip-off."

"I agree, Brody. I personally think it should have said 'guess the price and win a prize.' I believe they totally misled people by the way they phrased it. As I looked at the prints I had won I had barely heard of the artists and did not recognize any of the prints. They were different pictures of European settings I was not familiar with. I was thinking I would probably be lucky to get fifty dollars for all of them."

Fiona was looking at Devlin with incredulity as he told his story.

"Then the assistant started telling me how wonderful the prints were. She said she knew I would love them. They all had different colors which meant they matched nothing, and she thought it was so exciting I would now own famous art prints. Plus they all came with a letter of authenticity. And if I wanted they could have them matted and framed for a minimal price," Devlin told the group snickering.

"I just kept rolling my eyes as the assistant kept extolling the importance of the prints I had won. I wished you had all been there to witness the spectacle. I knew when you heard what happened; you would be as outraged as I am. And when that man said only one other person had ever guessed the right amount, how misleading that was. Every person walked out of that art auction room thinking I had won the Picasso. Anyway, I told the woman I would take them with me. She rolled them up in a tube so I can carry them off the ship. But I have to tell you the art people are probably thrilled to have gotten rid of those prints."

"That is an incredible story, Devlin."

"Yes, it is, Fiona. And I had to give her my address so they can send the letters of authenticity to me. Tonight before you go to your cabin I want you to come look at them. I still believe you really were the winner. You can have some or all of them. I honestly do not know what I will do with them. I can mail you the authenticity letters when I get them."

"I have to be honest, Devlin. I have no need for them either and do not want them. Maybe you could donate them to some charity."

"That is a good idea. You know there is nothing wrong with running a contest like that. I just think it is wrong to mislead the people about the prize."

"I think we all are in total agreement about that," Brody said. "Now I think it is time to go to dinner. It is past 7:30 p.m., and I have had nothing to eat since lunch. I don't know how I missed my late afternoon snack but I think I will make up for it at dinner. I am thinking about having two entrees tonight. They are offering prime rib or lobster as the choices, but I want both of them."

"Well," Fiona said laughing, "having two entrees has not stopped you before. I think you also had two on the first night we met when Miriam and Emma were so loud and obnoxious."

"I believe you are right, Fiona. So let's go have dinner."

The evening passed very quickly. Fiona forgot about her upcoming cruise, and thus never mentioned it to anyone. They had a leisurely meal and never did make it to the talent show. They had seen those shows before and Fiona told everyone at dinner what she had seen that afternoon at the tryouts. They all felt confident they could write about it in their articles.

After eating they went to the piano bar for the last

time and had after dinner drinks. Considering the egos that could have been involved, Fiona knew how special it had been that they all had gotten along so well. Actually much better than she had imagined. She felt she would be leaving old friends the next morning and hoped perhaps they could all get together sometime in the future.

As they said goodnight and good-bye at their cabin doors Fiona knew she probably would not see anyone in the morning. They would all be rushing off as soon as possible to catch their planes home. She, however, would take her time. She was looking forward to seeing how Miriam was faring. Fiona hoped she was not taking her mother's death too hard.

Chapter Seventeen

Sleeping in the next morning, Fiona awoke when she heard the announcement that anyone walking off the ship could now disembark. True to her cabin steward's word all her laundry had been cleaned and was lying on her bed when she returned from the piano bar the previous evening. She finished packing her suitcase and put the numbered tag the ship had given her around the handle. Then she had placed her bag outside the door before she went to bed.

In the morning after docking the luggage would be taken off and put in the ship terminal in specific areas. The special numbered tags determined what order you disembarked. Since she was not flying home and had no pressing reason to get off quickly, Fiona knew she would be one of the last numbers called to go ashore.

As she walked down the hallway to go to the buffet for breakfast she saw the rooms the others had been in were now empty since their doors were propped opened. She was glad she had said good-bye the evening before. After getting her food she sat on the outside deck eating while watching the passengers depart the ship.

Glancing over to the other side of the deck Fiona saw the table where she and Devlin had sat on the first afternoon of their cruise. She remembered how everyone had found them sitting there and started thinking about how much had happened to them since that first day. It had definitely been no ordinary cruise. But each one of her cruises always seemed unique in its own way.

Finally everyone was asked to leave the buffet area. The staff needed to get everything cleaned and ready for lunch before the next group of cruisers came aboard. This was the busiest day for the crew. They had to say a quick good-bye to over three thousand travelers and in about four hours be ready to greet another three thousand. Fiona marveled at how well the system worked.

Tomorrow she would be a part of another greeting as she sailed south to Key West and Progresso.

Before going back to her stateroom she stopped at the purser's desk. There was a fax that had come in with all the information on her Miami hotel, new cruise ship, and her flight home. Jordan's secretary had gotten everything put together for her, and now all she had to do was wait until it was time to disembark the ship. Since the weather was warm, but not too humid, Fiona sat on her balcony with the cabin door open so she could hear the announcements. It was not very long before she heard her number called and taking her carry-on she left the ship.

After picking up her luggage and going through customs she exited the cruise terminal and got into a waiting taxi. Fiona had been surprised that morning when she saw the name of the hotel where she was booked. She realized it was the same place where Miriam was staying. At least she would not have to worry about traveling too far around the city to locate her.

Luckily, even though it was only 11:00 a.m. when she got to the hotel, her room was ready. Sometimes you had to wait until 3:00 p.m. for your room because the maids were so busy cleaning rooms on the days the cruise ships were in port. But this was off-season so not as many people were in town as would be the case during the height of the season.

Fiona called Miriam's room but not getting an answer, she decided to go out. There were a lot of upscale shops in the area and she enjoyed window shopping along with walking in the warm temperature. She knew the thermometer would be lucky to hit forty today in the north.

About a block ahead of her Fiona saw a stretch limo pull up in front of a clothing store. A thirty something man dressed in white pants and a blue blazer exited the building carrying quite a few packages. Much to her surprise Miriam followed him out carrying even more packages. She tried to get Miriam's attention but she was too far away for the woman to hear her especially with the street noises all around.

Fiona continued to walk in the area for another hour and then stopped at a restaurant for lunch. She knew she was spoiled after being on the ship and eating constantly. Normally she might have skipped lunch but today she ordered a grilled chicken salad and ice tea since her walk had stimulated her appetite.

Returning to the hotel there was no message waiting. She called Miriam's room once again hoping she could catch up with her. Since there was still no answer, she left a message. She wondered if the woman was still out in the stretch limo shopping. So much for missing her mother, she mused.

Since she was not tired and did not want to walk outside anymore, she decided she might as well get busy and work. She had an idea for a couple of different articles about life aboard a cruise ship especially relating to the one she had just been on. Firing up her computer she was soon busy researching and writing about her recent experiences.

So lost in thought as she sat writing she jumped with the sound of the phone ringing in the quiet room. Looking at the clock beside her bed she was astounded when she saw it was 7:00 p.m. Picking up the phone, she heard Miriam's voice.

"Hi, Fiona. How come you are here in the hotel? Are you checking up on me?"

Laughing at Miriam's words she said, "I have better things to do then check up on you. Why in the world would you even think that, Miriam?"

"I am sorry. That was not a nice thing to say. I am sitting here worrying about my mother's disappearance, and sometimes I have the feeling I am being watched."

"That is pretty strange. I just wanted to call you and see how you were doing. Everyone left the ship and flew home this morning, but my editor asked me to do a follow up cruise since I was already down here. I leave tomorrow for five nights to Key West and Progresso."

"Don't you mean Cozumel?"

"No, this is a special sailing to Progresso/Meridia. It is on a different line than the ship we were on, but the same shipping company owns the line. Now tell me all about the young man I saw you with today? He was handsome but seemed a little young for you."

"What are you talking about? I was not with any young man. I have been in my room sleeping off a migraine all day. I turned the ringer on the phone down, so I did not hear your calls. I just woke up and saw the message light flashing."

"That is really strange. I could have sworn I saw you with lots of shopping bags and a youngish man getting into a stretch limo at lunch time when I was out walking. If it was not you, your double is here in Miami Beach."

"Are you accusing me of lying?"

"Of course not. The woman was a half a block away from me. She just looked so much like you; I just assumed it was you. Since I was here in town staying overnight, I really wanted to call and see how you were holding up, and if you had heard any word about your mother. Would you like to go out for dinner or a drink tonight?"

"Thanks. That is very thoughtful of you. I have not heard anything more about my mother. I am really not feeling very well tonight, so I would prefer to stay in my room and order in food. Maybe we can catch up with each other another time. But I really appreciate you calling me."

"Well, if you ever need someone to talk to, feel free to ring me. I just can't tell you how bad I feel about your loss."

Fiona heard the phone click and was surprised by Miriam's brusqueness. Since she had accomplished quite a bit on her article but still wanted to do a little more, she thought take-out was probably a good idea. Calling for room service, she ordered her favorite fish dinner in Florida...grouper.

Meanwhile, sitting at the desk in her room, Maxine heard a knock on her door and stood up. As she opened the door a thirty something man with a seventies style leisure suit eyed her low cut black cocktail dress. After kissing him she smiled. Then she turned and took a last look at all the shopping bags strewn all over her hotel suite.

Chapter Eighteen

Fiona finally quit writing and turned off her computer when the room service waiter arrived with her dinner. Turning on Fox News to catch the day's happenings she ate the food that had been delivered. She did not eat much at home mainly because she had to fix it herself and she tried to watch her weight. Being on a cruise ship with food always available tended to spoil you for real life.

Wondering how Miriam was doing she thought the woman was probably having a quiet evening eating alone in her room as she was doing. After she finished her meal, finding nothing interesting on television, she took a leisurely bath and went to bed to read.

Sometimes she stayed up quite late reading but, for some reason, tonight she found her eyes closing after just a few pages. Deciding to give in to her drowsiness she turned off her light and quickly fell asleep.

The next morning she could not believe it was almost 9:00 a.m. when she awoke. She had slept almost ten hours! Maybe all the emotional happenings of the last few days had caught up with her. She remembered having a vivid dream about Devlin and they were kissing. When she woke up she felt an emptiness and sense of loss that she would never see him again.

Shaking the lethargic thoughts away she got up and called room service for coffee and toast. I am sure getting spoiled she thought to herself. Coffee delivered to my room every day. What will I do when I go home and have to make my own coffee?

She turned on the television to Fox news to catch up on the latest happenings. Before long there was a knock on the door. Her coffee had arrived. Drinking the strong brew while checking her emails the morning passed quickly. The hotel had a shuttle bus to the terminal, and at 11:30 a.m. she found herself sitting in the lobby waiting for her ride. However this time there was no Devlin waiting in the lobby to go with her.

Chiding herself for even thinking about him she realized she had to let thoughts of a romantic encounter with Devlin go. It was not long before the shuttle pulled up and six other people climbed on board with her.

Smiling to herself, she heard the excitement of the three couples about their upcoming journey. I also get enthused when I think of my cruises and hope I never get over that feeling. It was very apparent one of the couples was on their honeymoon, and she wondered how much sightseeing they would actually do.

Soon they were pulling up to the cruise ship terminal, and the process of checking-in began. Just like the last time, she was directed to the VIP line, and this time she was escorted to an awesome suite on the top deck. Fiona was told that there were three other suites on the deck, but since this was the slow season only one other suite would be occupied. She wondered if it would be a honeymoon couple.

Entering her stateroom she was awe struck by the lavishness. She had never stayed in one of these suites and this particular one was absolutely spectacular. She had a huge living room which included a piano, a full size bar with stools, and a dining room table and chairs that overlooked a deck with her own hot tub. There were two bedrooms, and the master bedroom had a king sized bed and a balcony with windows that ran the whole length of the room. The suite also came with a butler who would be positioned right outside her door for assistance twenty four hours a day. This was opulence beyond belief.

Besides the two dining rooms and buffet the ship had five private dining rooms with different cuisines. There was always an additional cost to these specialty restaurants, but she was informed she had a standing reservation with no cost at any restaurant she chose while on the cruise. Fiona knew the food was always of much better quality in the specialty restaurants and decided she would skip the main dining room on this cruise. This was a luxury she would never have given herself on her own, so she knew she needed to avail herself of this extravagance since it was free.

Deciding to start enjoying the amenities immediately, she rang for the butler and ordered soup and salad for lunch. Her suitcase was delivered before her food, and she spent a few minutes unpacking. Knowing suitcases would not be delivered for another couple of hours to any of the other guests; she realized she could easily get used to living in this lap of luxury.

After sleeping so long the previous night, Fiona was not tired but she also did not feel like working right away. Putting on her swimming suit she relaxed in the hot tub for a while. After she dressed she knew she needed to do a little research on Key West since it had been quite some time since she had been there. Fiona knew there would be plenty of time to sit in her deck chair reading.

Since she would be alone on this cruise, she had stopped at the gift shop in the lobby of her hotel before leaving and picked up a book before departing for the ship. Once they got under way she could always go to the ship's library if she needed more reading material.

There was a lounge one deck down from her suite. Fiona had her butler make a reservation for 7:00 p.m. in the steakhouse restaurant that evening. The lifeboat drill would be at 5:00 p.m., and she had decided to go to the lounge for a glass of wine when the ship sailed instead of fighting the crowds down where the 'sailaway' party would be going on.

Fiona's butler's name was Morgan, and he told her he would be in charge of both suites. She learned from him that the other suite was also occupied by a single person, and therefore his boss felt he could handle both cabins. Under normal circumstances one butler was assigned to one suite, but since this was the off-season and with only one person in each suite the hotel manager was confident Morgan could handle whatever was needed for the two passengers.

Morgan showed her where the life jackets were kept. He then opened the door to the hallway and pointed out the private elevator that would take her to her muster station for the drill. He told her he would be taking a short break but would come right away if needed. All she had to do was ring the buzzer by the entrance door. Otherwise, he would be back on duty just before the drill to assist her to the elevator.

Looking up Key West on her computer, she began writing a preliminary draft of an article about what she had read. The island had less than thirty thousand people who lived there. In the past it had been a haven for writers and artists such as Ernest Hemmingway, Tennessee Williams and Robert Frost. Since the island was only ninety miles from Cuba naturally it was a refuge for Cuban political exiles. Coming south from the Florida mainland the scenic Overseas US Highway 1, ended in Key West. This made the island the southernmost spot in the contiguous United

States.

The island had also served as a base against pirates as well as a large salvage business from the many shipwrecks in the area. In the evening, just before sunset, people would flock to Mallory Square to watch the various street performers. Musicians, jugglers and contortionists would vie for the attention and donations of the spectators gathered to watch them.

After finishing her research Fiona sat in her deck chair reading, and the afternoon passed quickly and peacefully. Before she knew it the bells for the lifeboat drill were ringing. Fiona grabbed her lifejacket and went out her door to the elevator. She saw a man coming out of the door of the suite adjacent to hers.

To her shock and amazement, as the man turned towards her, she realized it was Devlin. What a serendipitous moment. And seeing Devlin's jaw drop, she realized he was as surprised as she was by the encounter. Was this a lucky break or the worst thing that could happen to the two of them?

Chapter Nineteen

Oh, damn, what a bummer! My luck seems to be changing from bad to worse all at once, Maxine was thinking.

It was amazing how easily I was able to fool those stupid ship officials and the police. I should have been a famous stage actress. Emma always said her daughter had her to thank for her career, but I knew that was not true. Emma never realized what was going on until that last evening just before she went overboard. She had no idea Miriam had created a second personality until I told her just before pushing her over the railing. I don't know if she believed me or not, but I don't care. The beauty of the situation is Miriam has no knowledge of me or my actions, so she can't tell anyone we murdered her mother.

The only thing Emma did well was marry. Both of her husbands died young leaving her lots of money. I wonder if she helped either of them to their early demise. Once in awhile she would give Miriam an idea of a place or a story since she had travelled so extensively, but she never wrote a single word. I know she constantly said her daughter would have been nowhere without her, but Miriam became an outstanding travel writer all by herself.

Since she only gave ideas and never contributed a single word, how could she believe becoming a brilliant travel writer was only due to her help? Maybe the years she spent confining Miriam in the closet while she went out and partied helped to stimulate her imagination. She never knew one of her live-in boyfriends found her little girl in the closet and did unspeakable things to her one night.

For three months after the attack, Miriam never spoke. Emma became so frantic that she promised to never again lock her up, thinking the closet had scared her. Miriam never told her mother what had really happened. The live-in boyfriend left the following week after the attack, and since she was no longer being imprisoned, little by little Miriam came out of her shocked state.

Emma continued to brainwash Miriam about how worthless her life would be without her. And then she met Randy, the love of her life. There was no way to prove it but I always felt Emma was responsible for his death, and I know Miriam wondered, too.

Randy did not want Miriam's mother to know about their marriage plans. Emma tried to convince her daughter that he was a gold digger and only wanted her money. But, what money? A travel writer's salary wasn't enough to live on in her mother's circle.

I know keeping her plans secret from her mother was upsetting to the passive Miriam. But she did not want to spend her life living with her mother. She was so in love with Randy and wanted to be with him forever. She wasn't sure how she would stand up to her mother, but knew she would have to at some point.

With both of their salaries she and Randy would not have been rich, but they would have been very comfortable. Randy wanted to live in San Francisco instead of Los Angeles. He thought if they could get far enough away from Emma's reach, she could not run their lives. And he was probably right.

Miriam often wondered why, oh why, did he go to

San Francisco that night without her? Emma had made such a big deal about having Miriam stay in Los Angeles to take her to a doctor's appointment. She should have gone with Randy instead. He had said when he returned they would pack up and leave immediately. He had been able to transfer his job to the San Francisco office, and Miriam could have written her travel pieces in any city.

Instead, for some unknown reason, he was driving late at night on that coastal highway when a hit and run driver sent him off a cliff. If only Miriam had been with him, maybe he would not have been on that road at that particular time. But then what would have happened to me, Maxine thought. It was after Randy's death that I came to life.

All these years Miriam kept wondering if Emma had something to do with his accident. If she thought for a minute that she had, the mousy Miriam would have gone truly mad. It has been twenty-five years and she still misses Randy as if it were yesterday. I know her life would have been totally different if they had moved to San Francisco as they had planned. Maybe they would have had children. Miriam would definitely have raised her children differently than her mother had raised her.

Miriam still does not know what happened to Emma that night on the ship. She cannot believe she was responsible for her mother's disappearance. She keeps trying to remember exactly what occurred but to no avail. Emma was in her usual drunken foul mood. When she started in on Randy and how Miriam had been saved by his death, her mind went blank and I came out. Someone had to stick up for that poor creature. Obviously she could not do it herself. After years of emotional abuse she was too beaten down to make any kind of a stand. It's a good thing she doesn't know about me. She might lose all sense of reality if she realized I was a part of her.

Like Miriam I don't know if Emma was actually involved in Randy's death or not. But she kept harping and harping and Miriam got madder and madder. All she wanted her mother to do was to be quiet and leave her alone. When Miriam passed out and I became aware of what was going on, I rushed at Emma and covered her mouth with my hand, so I would not have to listen to her. She backed away from me terrified when I told her who I was. When she reached the railing, she tried to stop me but I pushed her over. Then there was silence...blessed silence. At the time I remember thinking Miriam and I would never have to hear her voice again.

Anyway, I have to start thinking only positive thoughts. I have never been close to any women, but after Emma went overboard Diana, and especially Fiona, were so kind. In another world we might have been friends.

Fiona was especially caring that night Emma was lost at sea. I was very brusque with her when I called her at the hotel in Miami. Thank goodness we won't meet again. I would hate for Devlin to tell her that he saw me out with Zack that night when I had told Fiona I was in my hotel room. I would not want her to think badly of me. But the chance of her finding out is slim since the two of them will probably never see each other again.

And, after all, it was Emma's fault. All Miriam's life, it had been Emma's fault. She kept her from Randy, her one true love and made us wear those terrible dresses whenever we were together. She would drink herself into oblivion and was such a mean drunk. We never had any peace until we could dump her into bed every night.

She would never let Miriam forget that everything she had was due to her. I know Miriam drank too much when she was around her mother, but that was to dull the pain. Now Miriam has retreated into her own little world and I have been having so much fun with Zack here in Miami. I don't feel the need to drink as much as Miriam did in the past. And with all the dancing I am doing I think I have lost a good ten pounds since all my clothes are now loose on me. I feel myself getting stronger and stronger every day. Maybe one day I can get rid of Miriam altogether.

It has been wonderful dancing the night away in the nightclubs here in Miami, while just sipping a little champagne. Shopping in the daytime has been so satisfying now that I have plenty of money and don't have to listen to Emma telling us what to wear. I hate that California condo we live in. When I get back there, I am going to put that place up for sale immediately. It should bring a tidy sum. I don't want anything around that will remind me of Emma. And the double indemnity from her life insurance will bring even more money.

I will travel the world. No more writing since I will be rich. I wonder if I can talk Zack into coming to Los Angeles with me. I'll bet he will like the nightlife there as well as all the famous people I will introduce him to. We can go out dancing every night of the week if he wants to or travel together anywhere in the world.

Sometimes Maxine was amazed that someone as good looking as Zack, enjoyed her company. She had no idea that Zack was an insurance examiner who was investigating Emma's disappearance. The insurance company would have to pay out a lot of money if the double indemnity clause held up. But for now all she could think of was her good fortune in meeting him and her good luck that the police had quit questioning her or rather Miriam.

Chapter Twenty

"Devlin, what are you doing here?"

"I guess I could ask you the same question. You never told me you were doing another cruise."

As they went down the elevator to their muster station she told him, "I did not find out until the afternoon of our last day on board. I was so busy getting my clothes cleaned and checking last minute details, that when you came to my door with Peter and Brody, frankly I just forgot. But what about you? You never said anything either."

"I did not know until even later than you. When I went to my room that evening after the piano bar, there was a message that I had a communiqué at the purser's office. All it said was to call my office before leaving the ship in the morning. When I called the next morning my boss asked me to do this cruise since I was already down here. He had already cancelled my flight, rebooked a new one and made a hotel reservation for me. I did not see you anywhere so I jumped in a cab and checked into the hotel. Like you, I needed to get my laundry and a few other things done."

Since they had reached their muster station and there was no talking, both of them were reflecting on this new development of being together.

Fiona's stomach was doing a flip-flop just being in such close quarters with Devlin. She could not believe they were on this cruise together, and apparently alone. She had always believed fate had a way of taking control when you least expected it. Her friend Kathy had always told her if she ever got a second chance for love to grab it. She would always say, "If it changes your life, let it."

But what was Fiona thinking? This man was seven years younger than she. He was still in his early fifties and she was almost sixty. He could not possibly be interested in her in a romantic way. Maybe she should figure out a way to leave this ship before she made a fool of herself.

And yet, I know my mother was right, too. She hated to see me live such a barren and empty life although those were her words not mine. After I left Jason, I always felt fulfilled with my career and did not feel I had an empty life. But ever since I met Devlin, something about him stirs my soul. I don't know what to do. I feel so confused. I just want him to take me in his arms and....why, oh why am I thinking these thoughts. I have to stop right now.

Meanwhile all kinds of conflicting emotions were running through Devlin as well. He had liked Fiona as a friend right from the start. But he did not want a romantic involvement with anyone. He was afraid to feel again. What if he fell in love with Fiona, and she died like Shannon. Logically he knew the chances of that happening were slim. But at the same time he was afraid to let himself feel again. Like Fiona, he wondered why fate had brought them together like this.

Finally the drill was over, and they went up the elevator to return to their suites.

"So what do you think of your cabin?"

"Cabin is not a word that does it justice. Talk about luxury. Even if I could afford it, I do not know if I would spend the money that a suite like this would cost. But, at the same time, it will be easy to let someone pamper us in the way we are going to experience."

"Yes, I have the feeling Morgan will take good care of us. Did he show you the small room he has near ours? Unless we are off the ship, he is on constant duty. If we ring, he will be there at a moment's notice."

"It almost seems too decadent. And are you aware our suites are connecting? Imagine the money it would take to have two suites the size we are living in."

Nodding his head at her last statement Devlin asked, "What are you doing for dinner tonight? It seems rather ridiculous since we know each other, to pretend we don't and eat separately."

"That might be pretty awkward. I was planning on going to the lounge that is just one floor down and have a glass of wine when the ship leaves port. I was not really up for all the noise and activity at the "sail away" party. Morgan made me a dinner reservation for 7:00 p.m. at the steakhouse."

"I guess 'great minds run in the same channel.' That is exactly the same plan I had. It is almost 5:30 p.m. Do you want to go for a drink about six? I can tell Morgan to cancel one dinner reservation and make the other for two?"

"That is perfect. Why don't you just knock on my door when you are ready?"

Saying good-bye to each other, they went into their suites. Fiona wanted to change her clothes. She was wearing beige pedal pushers and wanted to dress a little nicer for dinner. She still could not believe how excited she was being with Devlin on another cruise. And this time no one would be around to act as a chaperone. Now all she had to do was get her stomach to quit doing flip flops every time she saw him.

Telling herself to quit thinking about Devlin, it was not long before he knocked on her door. As she opened the door she began laughing.

"Devlin, we are both wearing the same clothes we wore the first night on our last cruise. I guess it will not be long until our Christmas outfits."

Smiling Devlin's heart skipped a beat as he looked at Fiona. It was going to be extremely hard pretending they were just friends. He hoped their conversation did not get stilted. He could feel a little tenseness in Fiona's demeanor and wondered if she was as attracted to him as he was to her.

It turned out they had a fun evening. On the previous cruise they always had the other writers around so they had never had a chance to talk about their personal lives. On this cruise it was only the two of them.

They entered the bar, and Fiona knew she would enjoy coming here throughout the cruise. It was a small intimate bar about mid ship, and over half of the room had picture windows looking out over the vessel and the sea. As they were sitting in the bar watching the ship leave port Devlin's cell phone rang.

"I forgot I still had it on. It will not be long before I lose service altogether. Excuse me, Fiona. I need to take this. It is my daughter calling."

Not wanting to eavesdrop she could not help but overhear the conversation. Devlin was talking to someone he called Molly. He was very excited about some news he was hearing. As he disconnected he turned the phone off and stuck it in his pocket. Turning towards her, he was grinning from ear to ear.

"Well that must have been good news. You are grinning like a Cheshire cat."

"It was. You will never guess. I am going to be a grandfather!"

A sharp pain cut through Fiona knowing she would never have a chance to be a grandmother, but then she let it go and with a smile gave Devlin's hand a squeeze. As she touched him, she was stunned to feel a shock course through her and quickly withdrew her hand. Devlin was so excited about his news; he never realized she had even touched his hand.

"Congratulations. I am so happy for you."

Knowing her words were sincere, he wondered briefly why she had never had children. But being so excited he quickly let the thought go. Relating several stories of his daughter growing up as well as how she met her husband, Greg, time in the bar passed quickly.

It was almost 7:00 p.m. when they made their way to dinner. On their way Devlin said something astounding to Fiona.

"Since I was in Miami Beach last night, I decided to check out some of the night life. You know those nightclubs are famous there and just watching the people and their attire can keep you occupied most of the night. Some of the outfits are so outrageous and would never be seen outside of Miami."

As Fiona nodded Devlin continued, "You will never guess who I saw. It was Miriam!"

Fiona's jaw dropped at Devlin's words.

"She had on a rather 'sexy' black cocktail dress and was with some guy who looked in his thirties. He was wearing one of those seventies style leisure suits. It was strange. She looked at me, but turned away quickly without acknowledging me. My drink arrived, and when I looked around a few minutes later I could not see her anywhere. I almost thought I had imagined it."

"You did not imagine it." Fiona told him about spotting Miriam shopping and the limo. She then told him all about the woman's call to Fiona, and how she said she was sick and staying in that evening. "I saw a thirty something man with her, too. It has to be the same man you saw. I do not know what is going on but I cannot imagine why she would lie to me like that. Who cares if she is out running around with a much younger man?"

"It is a mystery. Maybe we should look into it a little deeper after this trip is over."

Wondering if Devlin realized what he had just said, amazed Fiona. It is almost as if he believes we will be together after this cruise she was thinking.

Fiona, studying her menu, looked up at Devlin and was about to say something. Just then the waiter came to take their order, and her thoughts were diverted.

They had an enjoyable evening together, but neither one of them ate very much. Fiona's stomach was still doing flip flops, and she could sense the tenseness in their conversation. The undercurrent was definitely affecting their time together. Although she said nothing, Fiona knew that Devlin was bothered by his feelings towards her, too. She had a feeling he had loved once and whatever happened she sensed he was afraid to try again. She got the impression he did not want a relationship with her anymore than she wanted one with him. At least that was what she was trying to convince herself of.

When dinner was over they went to the piano bar for an after dinner drink. Neither of them said much to the other but enjoyed listening to the music being played. True to form there were not many people out this evening. Most people were tired from their traveling and the excitement of the first night on their cruise. Fiona was hoping Devlin would not ask her to dance. She was afraid of her feelings if he wrapped his arms around her. Luckily, he did not ask.

Tomorrow they would be in Key West. They had decided to go ashore together and take the Conch Tour Train. The trolley was a ninety minute narrative about the island, and the shuttle bus from the ship would drop them at Mallory Square where the tour began.

It would be a good overview of the island. After her earlier research Fiona knew they would be seeing both the old and the new Key West including Hemingway's house, the waterfront, and a stop at a sign that said they were at the southernmost point of the United States. After talking about the other places they should visit, they finished their drinks and walked back to their suites.

Fiona was having a hard time not imagining what it would be like to kiss Devlin. It had been such a long time since she had been kissed and she knew she had to quit thinking about such things. She did not want Devlin to know she was envisioning his lips on hers. And so rapidly saying good night, she closed her door quickly

Being so excited about the news of Molly's pregnancy, he hardly noticed Fiona's quick departure. Turning towards his door, he went into his suite with a broad smile on his face.

Chapter Twenty-One

Fiona awoke at 3:00 a.m. She had been having a dream of Devlin and her together in a jungle. There were so many conflicting feelings flowing through her and her stomach ached with desire. This is so crazy she thought. We are all wrong for each other. And she was having difficulty getting past the age difference between them which she realized was foolish. Sexual feelings were coursing through her that she had not felt in a long time. And, unbeknownst to her, Devlin was having similar feelings.

Devlin had not been able to fall asleep. He kept thinking about Shannon and their life together. However a disturbing thing was happening. He could not picture Shannon's face. Instead he kept seeing Fiona in his mind. Then he remembered his daughter Molly telling him that even though he had loved Shannon, at one point in time, he had to let her go and be happy with someone else again.

Devlin knew Molly was right when she said Shannon would be upset to know he had closed himself off to life. I guess I need to not count on what I lost, but on what is left, and move forward. It would not diminish what I felt for Shannon. I have continued with life and grown older. I am about to be a grandfather, and Shannon will always be that sweet younger woman I once loved.

Finally accepting that Shannon had died and that

he must try living again even with another woman, Devlin fell asleep with a peace he had not felt in years.

Meanwhile, Fiona was tossing and turning. She had always believed she was responsible for the events in her life and the paths chosen. Even when she had no control, in the greater scheme of things, she knew there was no such thing as coincidence. Disease could be cured, but fate could not. As to their age difference it was obvious Devlin was not concerned by that fact. Destiny had placed them on this ship together, and although she did not know why; she decided to let things unfold and see what happened.

If they became serious about each other, this would not be an illicit affair they would be involved in. Actually it was plain and simple lust, something she had not experienced for a long time. For some reason she and Devlin were meant to be together again. After her mother's death she realized there was no permanence to life. The time we are given to live is both a privilege and a gift. She realized she needed to be happy and make the most of the time left to her.

We cannot change the past. The only control we really have is how we react to the good or bad that life sends us. Our life is determined by our attitude towards those events. We are the ones who choose to be happy or not.

As Fiona was thinking about this, she decided to surrender to her conflicting thoughts. Outwardly calm and serene, the turmoil she was feeling inside was taking its toll on her. Slowly she gave in to the idea of what pleasure with Devlin might bring. Life was too short to miss one precious moment of happiness. She wanted to enjoy Devlin's company for the next few days and not worry about what might happen. It had been years since she had wanted to be with a man, and she decided to let events unfold as they may.

When she looked at her clock she realized it was 5:00 a.m. She had lost two hours of sleep. But like Devlin, a peace she had not felt in a long time fell over her. She did not know him really well, but she knew he was a kind and thoughtful man. He was constantly making her laugh, and she knew he was not at all like her ex, Jason. They had bonded as friends after their initial distaste for each other. Sexual feelings aside, she felt very compatible with him when they were together. She had the feeling they would always be friends. That was not something to take lightly.

Let the games begin she thought to herself. Since I am in charge of my happiness, I am going to have fun and see what develops. Life is too short to wake up with regrets. Maybe I am too old to be feeling what I am feeling, and maybe we are never too old to feel love and happiness with someone. I know I am going to take a chance and find out if the opportunity presents itself.

And with that settled Fiona quickly fell asleep with a smile on her face.

Not too long after that her peaceful sleep was interrupted by a loud knocking on her door.

"Miss Fiona, Miss Fiona, are you awake?" She could hear the words coming from outside her door.

With a groan she reached for her robe and putting it on opened her door. There was Morgan.

"Miss Fiona, I do not mean to disturb you but I brought you the coffee you requested for 7:00 a.m. so you can get ready for your day exploring Key West."

"Thank you, Morgan. I awoke in the middle of the night and had trouble getting back to sleep. Apparently I slept later than I wanted to this morning."

"I hope you are not upset with me for waking you, Miss Fiona."

"Not at all. This is perfect timing. I am planning

on meeting Mr. O'Neill for breakfast before we go tour the island."

Laughing at the butler's surprised look Fiona continued, "Oh, Morgan, I know you made us one dinner reservation last night, but I am sure you do not know but Mr. O'Neill and I work for different travel magazines. We were together on another cruise with some other travel writers just before this one. Our publishers asked us to do this cruise since we were already in the Miami area. Neither one of us knew the other would be on this ship. Imagine our surprise when we met going to the lifeboat drill yesterday."

"Well, that is a surprise, Miss Fiona."

Realizing there were undercurrents in Morgan's reply she knew saying anything more would probably add fuel to his thinking. After all there was nothing between the two of them. But that did not mean there might not be before the cruise was over.

"We will be leaving after breakfast, Morgan, so once you clean our suites you can count on some free time. We do not plan to be back until later this afternoon."

"I will make sure your freezers have plenty of ice, Miss Fiona. And I hope you and Mr. Devlin have a very nice day."

"Thank you, Morgan. You have a good day, as well."

With that the butler left her room. Fiona wondered if he would be on his way over to Devlin's to see what he could learn from him. Deciding it was not important Fiona put on her make-up and clothes. Taking a cup of coffee to her balcony she watched the scene unfolding below her.

Buses were lining up to take the passengers on shore excursions or into the downtown area. The ship terminal was on the other side of the island from the downtown area, so there was not a lot to see in this part of the city. It was a rather typical port area but she caught a glimpse of a few residential areas, too.

They had been told it was about a ten minute bus ride to where all the action was. She and Devlin had arranged to go to breakfast at 8:30 a.m. There really was nothing pressing for them today. They were planning on taking the Conch Tour as soon as they got downtown. The tours ran every half hour, so they did not need to worry about being there at a certain time. Today they intended to be on "island time." By having breakfast a little later this morning, they would miss the initial rush of travelers getting off the ship.

As she sat drinking her coffee Fiona thought a little more about her research the previous day on the Florida Keys. Henry Flagler, an industrialist, began building hotels in St. Augustine in the late 1800s. His goal was to turn that city into an exclusive winter retreat. However, the temperatures were not as warm in northern Florida as they were in the southern part of the state. So he began building hotels further south, eventually all the way to Key West. However, there was just one problem; getting tourists to the island.

Flagler had started a railroad which stretched from the Northeast states to St. Augustine, to get his hotel guests to that city. Next he laid the railroad track that became the roadbed that put the Keys in easy reach. He could then use the railroad to transport the wealthy Northerners to his Southern hotels. Eventually a two lane road was built, which stretched one hundred thirteen miles on US Highway 1, from the Florida mainland down to Key West. It was a marvel in the making with forty two bridges connecting the different islands. Key Largo (made famous by the Humphrey Bogart film and in song) was the island next to the Florida mainland in the upper keys. The road ended at Key West.

The island reminded her of a coastal New England town but with the lush vegetation found on many Caribbean islands. As she looked towards the city she could see palm trees, hibiscus, and bougainvillea. She had read the architecture was predominately Bahamian, and the ship captains' had used wooden pegs instead of nails to build their homes. Living in a salty environment they did not have to worry about the rust and corrosion that comes with using nails. Today tourists flocked to the area for the beautiful sunsets and nightlife, as well as margaritas and key lime pie.

Interrupted from her thoughts, Fiona heard a knock on her door and saw Devlin's smiling face as she opened it. Something seemed different in his demeanor, but she could not quite put a finger on it. Letting the thought go, she grabbed her key card and followed him to the stairs that led to the buffet.

"Breakfast on the outside deck of a ship is getting to be a habit."

"You're right. It seems like we have been doing this together for ages. It will feel strange when I go home and have breakfast alone in my kitchen, much less start making my own coffee again."

Smiling she told him she had the exact same thought this morning.

"I had another idea for today and wondered if you might be interested."

"What is that?"

"Usually the cruise ships are only in port here in Key West until mid afternoon. But since we have the special sailing to the Yucatan to be closer to the ruins, we will be here until 10:30 p.m. tonight. I know you are aware of that. I was thinking we could come back to the ship sometime this afternoon when we are finished touring and have an early dinner, maybe just a quick one at the buffet, and then return downtown. We could see the sunset, but more importantly, I thought it might be fun to take the 'Ghosts and Legends Tour' of the Old Town area."

"I had not really thought about that, but you are absolutely right Devlin. We have always left this island in the mid afternoon to get to Cozumel. That ghost tour would probably be a really fun thing to do since we are here so late. If nothing else, it will certainly give us some new information for our research. In addition it will be terrific to see one of their famous sunsets here."

"I was reading about the ghost tour, and we can make reservations when we are in town this morning. The first tour is at 7:00 p.m. and lasts about ninety minutes. That gives us plenty of time to get back to the ship. We could even stop and have a drink at Jimmy Buffet's Margaritaville before returning to the vessel."

"Let's do that. I need to go grab a sweater in case we run into some cool air. I know the tram is open air but sometimes I get a chill going into stores with the air conditioning turned up high."

The two of them stopped back in their rooms briefly to get what they needed for the day. Morgan was already hard at work cleaning Fiona's suite. She told the butler their plans for the day. He seemed pleased that he would have some time off. Often he was very busy with one suite, much less two, but he had the feeling this would be an easy cruise for him.

Looking around one last time to make sure she had not forgotten anything, Fiona opened the door of her cabin and saw Devlin coming out of his stateroom at the same time. Smiling at each other the two of them set off for whatever adventure awaited them on this day in paradise.

Chapter Twenty-Two

The sun was shining brightly as Fiona and Devlin went down the gangplank to board a bus for the downtown area. As they arrived at the Square the two of them truly believed they had arrived in paradise, albeit a bustling one. The flowers and vegetation could only be described as truly lush.

The tram was just getting ready to pull out as they went to the small booth to buy tickets. They were told the one presently leaving was already sold out. However, there were tickets available for the next tram leaving in a half hour. So they purchased their tickets separately and decided to look in the shops around the Square.

Laughing, Devlin said, "For two non-shoppers we have certainly spent a lot of time in stores lately."

"You are right about that, but it is good to know what kinds of things they sell to the tourists for our articles."

"Do you think they have different things than the Bahamas?"

"Yes, I do. There is always the regular tourist 'stuff'. But this island is American and with the famous writers and artists who have flocked here, I think there is a better quality of paintings and even clothes."

Devlin just continued laughing and shaking his head as they entered another store.

Finally, looking at her watch she said, "I think our shopping time is over. We need to get to the tram, so they don't leave without us."

"I can't say I am not happy to hear those words."

It was not long before their tour was over, and sharing a sandwich they went to check out the Hemmingway house. The mansion was built in 1851, and Hemmingway bought it in 1931. The lush tropical garden, planted by the author, was home to more than fifty cats descended from the author's felines.

"They certainly do not need to worry about rats or mice getting into this house."

"No. And did you see that penny embedded in the concrete at the head of the pool? He supposedly did that when he found out what the pool would cost to install, Fiona."

"You know I can almost see him sitting at his desk in that house writing 'For Whom the Bell Tolls' watching his cats running around in the yard."

"Maybe you will really see him in there tonight when we are on the ghost tour."

Laughing at that, the two of them went back to the Square to catch a shuttle bus to the ship. Since the island had been very humid that day, they both headed for their showers and changed clothes before going to the dinner buffet. Neither one of them had seen Morgan, but they had no need for him, so had not rung their buzzers. They knew their bathrooms would be freshened up and their beds turned down on their return.

It was not long before they were getting back on the shuttle bus for the ride downtown. At 7:00 p.m. sharp they were back in a tram listening to stories and legends about haunted mansions, pirates and voodoo superstitions.

"I have never been on one of these ghost and legend

tours before. Lots of cities, especially in the south, have them. Even though I do not believe the stories, it is fun to hear them."

"You are just disappointed you did not see Hemmingway at his desk writing," Devlin said while chuckling once again at something she said.

"Well that was a disappointment. Anyway let's go over to Jimmy Buffet's now and have a margarita. They have take-out cups and we can go out in the street with all the other tourists and watch the sunset."

By 9:00 p.m. they had finished their drinks, and the last pinks and oranges were seen in the sky as they boarded the shuttle bus for the ride back to the ship.

It had been a fun and productive day for both of them. Tired and a little worn out from the humidity they said goodnight at the door of their suites promising to meet for breakfast in the morning. Tomorrow they would be heading towards the Western Caribbean and new adventures.

Fiona smiled as she entered her suite. Her bathroom had been cleaned and her bed turned down. Towels, shaped like an elephant, were placed at the bottom of her bed. After showering she put on her nightgown deciding it was going to work out well to let things unfold in their own fashion. She was asleep five minutes after her head hit the pillow. Today had been a relaxing day with none of the tension she had felt the previous day. Maybe tomorrow would be a different story.

Chapter Twenty-Three

Fiona had a small private balcony off her bedroom. She had opened the door when she retired on the previous evening. The warm breezes of the tropics were blowing her curtains the following morning as she awoke. She and Devlin had not made any plans to meet for breakfast, and she decided to have Morgan bring her a tray so she could relax on her patio out by her hot tub.

Exiting from her bedroom to the living area after dressing, she opened the door to the patio. Although there was a folding wall barrier between the two suites, there was a space in between and Fiona could hear noise coming from the other side.

"I believe I hear you over there, Devlin."

"Yes, you do."

As she watched, the wall partition suddenly swung opened, and Fiona saw Devlin dressed in shorts and a T-shirt, standing there. She also saw a tray with food and coffee on his patio table.

"Great minds, I guess. I just asked Morgan to bring me a breakfast tray, too."

"Why don't you come over and have a cup of my coffee while you are waiting for your breakfast to arrive?"

"Thanks. I would love to. What is on your schedule for today?"

"I really did not think I would do too much. I

wanted to get some notes down on Key West and do a little research on the Yucatan Peninsula and the Mayan ruins. Then this afternoon I was going to read. I am really not very interested in the shipboard activities. They are pretty much the same on all ships. Since we were just on the Bahamas cruise, we have definitely seen enough to write our critiques."

"Doing research is exactly what I planned for the day, too."

"Let's have breakfast together and then go our separate ways. Would you like to have lunch in the dining room??"

"That would be perfect, Devlin. How about 12:30 p.m.? It will make for a nice break."

It was not long before she heard Morgan bringing her breakfast tray out to her patio.

"Bring it over here please. Devlin and I are going to have breakfast together," she told the butler.

As she put the cup of coffee, she had taken from Devlin, down the butler brought her tray over to where the two were seated.

"That is perfect. Thanks Morgan. Devlin and I were running out of coffee, and you came just in the nick of time."

Neither of them noticed the strange look the butler gave them as he left the suite. They chatted while they had breakfast, and then Fiona went back to her suite after finishing. Devlin was on his way to the library to do some research. But before he left he closed the folding door between their patios, so they could both have their privacy. Fiona smiled at his thoughtfulness as she heard him leaving his cabin.

Having been to the ruins of Tulum previously, she

was looking forward to Chichen Itza since she had never been there. She knew the ruins they were going to visit were the best preserved of all the Mayan ruins. They were even listed as one of the "Seven Wonders of the Modern World," and she wanted to read up on them before they arrived at the site. Since this was a day at sea, it was perfect for going over the research papers she had printed out at her hotel in Miami before coming on the ship.

It was not long before she was immersed in her readings of the ruins and culture of the ancient Mayans. Fiona had always been a visual learner, so the first thing she did was look at a map of the Yucatan Peninsula. Although the peninsula was a part of Mexico, the people who lived there considered themselves Yucatecos first and Mexicans second.

Evidence of the ancient Mayan civilization on the Yucatan dated back to early 400BC; although Chichen Itza had been dominant from 600 AD to about 1200 AD. Even though the city had collapsed around 1200 AD, there was still a thriving local population living there when the Spaniards arrived in the early 1500's.

Mexico was comprised of states just like the United States, and the Peninsula contained three. At the top was the state called Yucatan. The capitol city of Merida was located about twenty-two miles inland and had a population of around one million four hundred thousand people. The cruise ship would dock in the town of Progresso where the longest pier in the world had been completed in 2001. The waters of the Gulf of Mexico were so shallow in the area that cruise ships had been unable to stop at the port in the past. Now it would be a simple bus ride to Merida on a four-lane highway to get to the road leading to the ruins.

Merida was a very unusual city for Mexico or even the Caribbean. The town was extremely proud of its reputation for cleanliness. In many foreign countries trash was thrown all along the roads and neighborhoods, and considering how many people lived in Merida the town had a right to be proud of their accomplishment. For Mexico it was also a very cosmopolitan city and rivaled many that were found in South America.

The city had been founded in 1542 on the site of an ancient Mayan city. The cathedrals, ornate mansions and parks had been built over the crumbling remains of the temples and palaces, and much of the ancient stone had been used to build the new city.

Merida had become even wealthier in the last half of the 19th century when it was discovered that a tough thorny plant, henequin, a member of the agave family; thrived in the rocky soil.

Large plantations had used Indian field workers to extract the fibers from the leaves by hand. Later machinery had replaced the workforce. The fibers were used for a variety of products such as twine, burlap sacks, furniture stuffing and hammocks. By World War I the city had more millionaires per capita than any other city in the world, but was still considered a backwater full of mosquitoes.

The wealthy, trying to change their image, began building Moorish style mansions with arched doorways and marble tile interiors. These mansions lined the boulevard that led into the city. Today the mansions were no longer privately owned but had become businesses like banks, restaurants, hotels and bed and breakfasts. There were very strict building codes, and the homes had to retain their historic look and colors no matter who owned them.

But Merida's importance now was due to the fact that it was a jumping off point to the most important of the Mayan ruins, Chichen Itza. From the cruise ship it was a forty-five minute ride to the city and then about an hour and a half past there to the archeological site. Because the ruins were something she and Devlin had never been to before, they had both signed up for that shore excursion.

The second state on the peninsula was Campeche, and the capitol had the same name as the state. It was located just south of Merida on the west side of the peninsula on the Gulf of Mexico. Fiona's research indicated that the waterfront there was dotted with off-shore oil rigs, but its importance was due to Mexico's gulf coast shrimp fleet located in the town.

Campeche was also famous for its one and a half mile wall that was erected to protect the town from the pirates that used to try and sack the area. Fiona had previously read about Jean Lafitte the famous pirate who was driven from New Orleans and later Galveston Island. No one knew how he died.

Lafitte had made many trips to Campeche and was reported to have been headed to that area when the United States Army drove him out of Galveston. After he departed Texas he had literally sailed off into history and was never heard from again. Many thought perhaps a hurricane had sunk his ship, because no one had seen or heard from him in Campeche after he had been driven out of the United States.

Finally, the third state in the Yucatan on the east side of the peninsula located on the Caribbean Sea was called Quintana Roo. Both Cancun and Playa del Carmen are in this state, as well as, Cozumel the island located directly east of Cancun.

Fiona had docked several times in Cozumel. A few years ago she had taken a shore excursion to some Mayan ruins that had really impressed her. They had taken a high speed ferry from the island to just south of Playa del Carmen. There is a very deep channel that separated

Cozumel from the mainland. After the ferry docked they had been bused for approximately forty-five minutes to the ruins of Tulum. The site had been unbelievable. The ruins are located right on the Caribbean Sea and the cliffs, over thirty nine feet tall, made the area a natural defense against invaders. In addition the surf had really been pounding the day she was there since the ruins opened to the sea.

The city was at its height between the 13th and 15th centuries and even survived well after the Spanish had occupied Mexico. Actually it was the diseases the Spaniards had brought that had done the city in. In its heyday, the town had a population of over fifteen hundred and it was sad to think they had been destroyed due to the white man diseases which had also been the fate of many American Indians.

Tulum had been so impressive, and Fiona had always heard Chichen Itza was even more awesome. Besides the New Seven Wonders of the World designation Chichen Itza was also a UNESCO World Heritage site. Visiting all the UNESCO World Heritage sites was on her "bucket list," and she hoped she could accomplish seeing them all in her lifetime.

It seemed amazing to her that, except for Tulum on the coast, all the other ruins were inland. The peninsula was a limestone plain which made for great building material. However there were no rivers or streams. Instead there were natural sinkholes called cenotes. Some of these were as deep as ninety feet. Archeologists concluded the Mayans had conducted sacrifices during times of drought. They had found jade and gold and even skeletons of children and men to support the theory that they had been thrown into the cenotes.

Fiona wondered if the Mayans did not consider themselves safer inland. They did not have to worry about marauders from the sea since their sites were not visible from the water. It also had to help being inland during times of natural disasters such as hurricanes. But no matter what the reason, she was excited to finally be able to see for herself the difference between the coastal and interior sites. Tomorrow the ship would arrive at Progresso at 7:00 a.m. and by 7:30 a.m. they would be on their way.

They had already asked Morgan to deliver breakfast to their rooms at 6:00 a.m. Neither of them felt bad about getting the butler up early because after they departed he would have the rest of the day free until their return sometime after 3:00 p.m.

Box lunches were provided on the seven and a half hour tour, so they did not have to worry about taking any food with them. Only large bottles of water, sunscreen and hats would be needed, as well as, sturdy shoes since there would be quite a bit of walking. The ruins were six miles square with hundreds of structures although the main core of the site where they would be taken was just less than two square miles. It certainly promised to be an interesting day.

As Fiona continued reading she heard a knock on the door. Looking up, she glanced at her clock and realized it was already 12:30 p.m. Where had the morning gone?

Answering her door she saw Devlin still in his shorts and T-shirt standing in front of her with a smile.

"Oh, my gosh. I cannot believe how late it is. I have been reading about the Yucatan, and I don't know where the time went. It certainly is a fascinating chapter in Mexican history."

"I am not sure about you, but I am starved! As if we don't get enough to eat on board ship. Are you ready to go get some lunch and compare notes?"

"Yes, I am definitely ready, too. But as far as getting enough to eat, I am definitely going light this afternoon. I think salad and some fruit will be all I need."

"That sounds perfect to me, also."

After they ordered their food Devlin began a very animated discussion of the Mayan culture. Fiona smiled to herself because it was a lot of the same information she had read that morning. However, she was happy to see how enthused he was about their upcoming adventure. Since the Mayans had come from Mongolia over thirty thousand years ago, it was exciting to be able to trace a couple of thousand years back.

"The only sad thing about our journey tomorrow is we will no longer be able to climb the monuments or go inside the chambers. In 2006 a woman from San Diego fell to her death climbing the pyramid and that, along with some other accidents, was the end of anyone being allowed to do anything except walk around the area."

"There is still plenty to see, Fiona. Did you know the El Castillo pyramid is ninety eight feet tall? It is astounding to think of those early people building such a commanding structure. And even though we are not allowed to climb the pyramid, there are still many other structures to check out."

As she nodded her head at what he was saying, he continued, "I am looking forward to seeing the Great Ball Court, the Temple of the Bearded Man, the Temple of the Jaguar and the Steam Bath. I realize El Castillo is the crown jewel of the site, but so many of the other structures have also been preserved or restored. It promises to be a very interesting day."

"What did you learn about El Castillo?"

Devlin happily continued sharing what he had read that morning. "It is also called the Temple of Kukulkan which is a Mayan feather serpent deity. It is amazing how the Mayans were into math and science so far back; very comparable to what the Greeks were discovering about the same time."

He resumed, "The Mayans, however, used the number 0 while the Greeks did not. And their calendar was amazing. Actually the calendar works within a couple of circles, one being a twenty-eight day moon cycle and the other much bigger. Every fifty-two years the Mayans go through a new cycle.

Recently there had been talk about the Mayans predicting the end of the world. But that was totally not true. December 21, 2012 was actually the end of the twelfth cycle. This latest calendar has been going on for six hundred twenty four years. On December 22, 2012, a new cycle began. It is the thirteenth cycle. The Mayan descendants believed since it is the start of a new cycle, it signals a new beginning for mankind; a chance to start again, and hopefully a peaceful and prosperous time for all."

Not realizing Fiona had also researched Mayan history, he continued talking about what he had learned. "You probably know the pyramid has four sides to signify the four seasons. In the 1930's the government sponsored an excavation, and after a few false starts they found another temple buried under the current one. Imagine finding a lost temple, and inside was a throne shaped like a jaguar painted red with spots made of inlaid jade. Even though it is closed to the public now, it sounds like something out of an Indiana Jones adventure."

Listening intently to him she added, "And speaking about math, did you know the pyramid consists of three hundred and sixty five steps to symbolize the days in a year?"

"I did not know that. But whenever you see pictures of the site, El Castillo is the predominate building. This is where all the people come for the spring and autumn equinoxes. Along the northwest corner in the late afternoon on those two days a series of triangular shadows are cast on the pyramid that give the appearance of a serpent wriggling down the staircase. It is hard to imagine, with the technology of that time, building something so precise. Some people think it was supposed to represent the feathered serpent god Kukulcan, but that has never been substantiated. It sure would be fun to come back and visit during an equinox some time."

"I was thinking the same thing. I know there will not be any time to spend in Merida, but I would like to return and explore that city some day, too. I know I would enjoy returning here. There is so much to see, including Campeche. I could easily spend a couple of weeks going to all the other Mayan sites on the peninsula. It would make a great travel article."

"Would your editor let you do something like that?"

"Normally he gives me my assignments, although I am allowed input. But I was thinking when I hand in my article on Chichen Itza, I would tell him my idea for more articles on the Mayan ruins. He would never say 'yes' right away, but after thinking about it for a while he would probably conclude it would make for a great story. By the time he assigned it to me, it would be his idea. But who cares. At least I could come back and the magazine would pay for it."

"Since we are having a light lunch, how about an early dinner?"

"That sounds good. We could skip our pre-dinner glass of wine, and have it with dinner instead. Should we have Morgan make a reservation for dinner around 6:00 p.m.? We can have a leisurely meal and then turn in early."

"That is exactly what I was thinking. But I want to get back to my book now. I have been reading John Stephen's account of his travels on the peninsula, and it is fascinating. No wonder so many people started visiting the Yucatan after his book was published."

Saying good-bye at the restaurant door, the two of them went their separate ways. Fiona had scheduled a massage for later in the afternoon. She was looking forward to the relaxation a massage provided and hoped it would help her to go to sleep early that evening.

Before she knew it, she and Devlin were having dinner and saying goodnight. She could hardly wait for their adventure the following day. Little did she know it would be more than she ever imagined in her wildest dreams.

Chapter Twenty-Four

The sun was shining even though it was only 5:30 a.m. when Fiona's alarm went off. Once again it was another beautiful day in paradise she was thinking. She realized though it would be very warm and humid inland. Jumping in the shower was refreshing, but she knew she would be sweating as soon as she started walking among the ruins.

At 6:00 a.m. precisely there was a knock and as she opened the door Morgan came in rolling a cart containing two trays.

"Good morning, Miss Fiona. Where would you like me to put your breakfast?"

"Outside on the table will be perfect. Thanks, Morgan. I hope you have a nice day today. It should be peaceful with us gone on our shore excursion."

"Thank you, Miss Fiona. I know you will have a wonderful day, too. I was able to go on the tour a couple of years ago, and the ruins are quite impressive. Enjoy your breakfast and just leave everything as it is. I will be in to clean your suite as soon as you and Mr. Devlin leave."

"That is excellent. We plan to leave at 7:15 a.m. I see you have Devlin's tray with you. Do you mind telling him I will meet him in the hall at 7:15 a.m.?"

"I will do that, Miss Fiona."

As the butler departed Fiona went out and sat on her patio and poured a cup of coffee. With all the walking they would be doing that day she had decided on a light breakfast of a muffin, yogurt, and some fruit. Before she knew it the time to leave had arrived. As she went into the hallway she saw Devlin closing his door at the same time, and they smiled at each other as they took the elevator to the gangplank.

As they walked down the pier to the terminal they saw a sign that said Chichen Itza tour, and they gathered with the other travelers who were waiting there. Soon a man who was wearing a badge with the name, Temo, escorted them to the waiting bus. It held thirty five passengers, a little smaller than the big tour buses. Temo explained that once they left Merida they would be driving on two-lane roads, and a smaller bus was easier to maneuver in that area.

Devlin and Fiona were one of the first ones to board, and Fiona walked to the back immediately.

"You don't want to sit up front so we can hear better?"

"No, I prefer the back. We do not have to worry about people talking around us, and the guide uses a microphone. I don't know if you noticed, but there is a second exit door in the middle of the bus so we will not have to wait for everyone to get off. We can sit up front if you would rather."

"No, the back is fine."

As they drove towards Merida Temo gave them a history of the town, and the role the Mayans had played in the area. Basically none of the information they were given was new to them, but they were both enjoying the ride. They passed a swamp and Fiona saw an alligator swimming in the water. It made her wonder what other wildlife inhabited the area.

All too quickly they passed Merida, and as promised the road became two lanes and fairly narrow. They still had a good hour's ride ahead of them. Since they had skirted around the outer area of Merida, they had not been able to see any of the older part of town. Wistfully, Fiona hoped she would be able to come back and visit the area more in depth at a later date.

About fifteen minutes from the ruins they stopped at a souvenir/restroom stop. Fiona did not want any souvenirs, but after the drinks she had that morning she was ready for the bathroom break. Already the day was getting warm and humid and the air conditioning felt good when they reboarded the bus.

Knowing they had to adapt to the humidity Temo explained that there would be several groups with guides at the ruins. He did not want to lose his passengers. He had a hand held speaker that he would carry so everyone could hear his explanations, but he warned everyone to stay with the group and keep their eye on the orange sign he would carry in his other hand.

His sign was on a long stick, so when he held it up it was easy to see from a distance. He would give them some time later to explore some on their own, and then he would let them know when and where to meet him. As long as they looked for the orange sign they would not get lost or mixed in with another group.

Temo reminded everyone to take their bottled water. Once they arrived at the site everyone got off and started following the guide. Fiona did not think it was possible, but the ruins were even more impressive than Tulum. El Castillo was definitely as awesome as promised. It was a shame they could not walk up the steps of the pyramid.

Temo took them from one structure to the next explaining in depth about each place they were seeing. The two of them had done their homework on the area, but the guide personalized what they were seeing and added so much more than if they had been walking around on their own.

They followed the guide for an hour and a half, and Fiona could feel her body getting wet with sweat. She was sorry she had not brought a change of clothes with her, although she didn't know where she would have changed if she had.

After the guided tour they were given thirty minutes to roam around, and Temo showed them the path to leave the ruins when their time was up. He told them to meet him in the parking lot where he would be standing in the front of their bus, holding his orange sign up high, so they would find the correct vehicle. Then they would go back to the souvenir shop to use the bathrooms and eat their box lunches.

All too soon they boarded the bus and headed for their lunch stop. Devlin started laughing, as they sat at picnic tables to eat, when Fiona told him about needing a change of clothes.

"The good thing is everyone will be reeking of sweat, so maybe it won't be as offensive since we will all smell the same. We have almost a three hour ride back to the ship, so hopefully we can ignore the stink."

"At least it started clouding up about an hour ago, so we have not had to deal with the sun beating down on us. But this humidity is really oppressive. It almost feels like a bad storm is coming. Did you hear anything about rain in the forecast?'

"No, but at this point a little rain would feel pretty good."

Devlin had no idea how much he would regret those words later that night. A bad storm had been brewing, but the captain had not mentioned it to the passengers since he knew they were leaving Progresso a few hours before the squall would hit. The seas might be a little choppy but nothing like they would be if they got caught in the tempest.

Soon it was time to board the bus for the trip back to the ship. Fiona noticed they were the last bus to leave the parking lot. And, as predicted, everyone smelled pretty bad. However, the air conditioning felt wonderful and seemed to mask the smell somewhat. They had been driving almost an hour and were still a good half hour from Merida. Fiona noticed many of the passengers were dozing. Devlin seemed lost in his book when she heard a noise almost like gunfire, and the bus began to swerve. Thankfully the driver was able to stop before anything serious happened.

The driver was talking loudly in Spanish and Fiona wondered if he was swearing. He certainly did not look happy. The area they had stopped in was a little swampy to the left, although Fiona saw a village a little ways off to the right.

"Please everyone stay calm. At least Jorge was able to stop the bus and no one got hurt. The driver and I will be right back. We believe we have had a blow out, and we are going out to assess the damage. As soon as we know what has happened, we will call and ask for help. But I must ask you to stay on the bus. It is not safe out here with the swamp wildlife."

It was not long before Fiona saw Temo and Jorge out on the right side towards the back of the bus. Jorge was pointing and talking very agitatedly. I wonder how many swear words he knows Fiona thought to herself. Then she saw Temo get on his cell and start talking. Not too long after that the two men got back on the bus.

"Here is the situation, folks. We have had a blow

out, as we suspected. They will send a truck to tow the bus back to the shop as soon as they can. But with this being a cruise day there are no extra buses available right now. As soon as one of our buses drops passengers at the cruise ship it will turn around and come get us. But it will probably be two hours before the bus gets here and then another hour and fifteen minutes back to the ship. My company has called the cruise ship to tell them the news. With this being a ship sponsored shore excursion we have been assured the boat will not sail without you."

Everyone groaned at the thought of sitting on the bus for another two hours before help would arrive.

"Jorge can keep the air conditioning running, so you will be comfortable. Please relax and the time will go by."

Pulling out a book she had brought, Fiona looked at Devlin. "Thank goodness I brought something to read. I usually just like looking at the landscape but always bring a book along just in case."

"That was smart of you. I sometimes have to sit a long time at airports, and so I always carry one, too."

The two of them sat reading for about an hour. As they looked up at about the same time they noticed a small shape in the distance that kept getting closer to them. Soon they realized it was a little boy probably about three years old.

"He must have come from that village over there and wandered away from his mother."

Just then a woman in the front of the bus began screaming. A Burmese python close to sixteen feet long was headed for the child. There was nothing anyone could do except watch the unfolding scene with horror. The python, an ambush predator, had obviously staked out the trail watching for prey. The little boy had no idea what was happening. They could hear him crying presumably looking for home.

Out of nowhere a dog about forty-five pounds appeared and began barking loudly at the snake. Just behind the dog ran a woman. The dog's bark was enough to distract the snake from the child. The python seized the dog in its sharp backward-pointing teeth and crushed the animal with its weight as it coiled around it. The dog was dead before the python began to consume it whole. The snake could barely move as it slowly wiggled its way back to the brush of the swamp.

It was definitely the most gruesome thing anyone on the bus had ever seen. The only redeeming factor was that the dog had inadvertently saved the child's life. Everyone watched as the sobbing mother grabbed her son and ran back towards the village.

An eerie silence descended on the bus as the passengers wondered what kind of nightmares they would probably now have. As if coming out of a trance Fiona realized she was grasping Devlin's hand. As she looked at him with tears in her eyes, he leaned over and kissed her on the cheek.

It was another forty five minutes before the relief bus showed up, and Fiona never let go of Devlin's hand until it was time to move to the other vehicle. Everyone seemed fearful as they moved to the new bus wondering if there was another snake nearby ready to get one of them. It was a day no one would ever forget as long as they lived.

Not a word was spoken on the way back to the ship. When they got to the terminal everyone gave Temo and Jorge tips as they exited the bus. The two men nodded their thanks. However there was no laughing or joking as usually happened at the end of a shore excursion. They showed their picture IDs to the security guard, and ship personnel quickly walked them down the pier and onto the boat.

They knew they were two and one half hours late, but had no idea there was any significance to that fact.

Chapter Twenty-Five

Fiona and Devlin took the private elevator up to their suites. The air had become very oppressive and even the water looked roiled up. It was almost as if the sea was upset because the dog had lost his life.

"I don't know about you Fiona, but after I shower and clean up I need a stiff drink."

"A drink sounds good, but I don't want to sit outside. Why don't we get cleaned up and go to the bar?"

"I'll let Morgan know we are going for drinks and we can worry about what to do for dinner later. Is that all right with you?"

"That will be fine. I'm not sure how hungry I will be tonight, but right now a drink will hit the spot."

"Don't worry. We'll play it by ear. First I need a shower to feel clean again, and then a drink. We can take it from there after that."

Fiona realized Devlin had not said anything about her holding his hand all the way back to the ship. She did not know why she had done that, except she just wanted to feel some human contact after watching the horrible scene with the snake. It had certainly been a gruesome way for the dog to die, but thank God it had not been the little boy. She tried to erase that thought from her mind.

As she got into the shower she felt the dirt and

sweat from the day wash off of her. If only she could remove her thoughts that easily. She stood under the spray for a good ten minutes, and then feeling guilty for wasting so much hot water she finally turned it off. As she stepped out of the shower she heard the bells ringing for the captain to speak. That was pretty odd. Usually the captain only gave a daily report at noon about the weather conditions. I guess he wants to explain why we are running so late she was thinking.

"Good evening, Ladies and Gentlemen. This is your captain speaking from the bridge. I know many of you realize we had a problem with a bus breaking down on a shore excursion this afternoon. Because of that we are running about two and a half hours late this evening. Normally we could make a lot of that time up. I do not anticipate any trouble but I want everyone to know there is a bad storm we may run into tonight due to our late departure from Progresso. Please do not be alarmed. We may have some rough seas for awhile, but we have a sturdy vessel and should have no problems. I just want you to be aware that it could get a bit nasty. We will definitely keep you informed if there are any other updates. Tomorrow is looking very good with fair skies and warm temperatures. I hope you all have a very pleasant evening."

Just then Fiona heard her phone ring.

"It's me, Fiona. How close are you to that drink?"

"I will be ready in ten minutes. Do you want to knock on my door or should we meet in the hall?"

"I'll just knock, and then you will know I am ready."

"That's fine. You know, I am wondering how much more we can take today. As you are aware I have been on a lot of cruises and the captain has never come on with an announcement like that before. I wonder if we should be concerned about the weather?"

"Don't worry about something you cannot control. We made it through this afternoon, and we will make it through tonight."

Fiona was not as sure as Devlin seemed to be. But at this point there was nothing anyone could do about the developing situation. The ship was now on a course back to Miami, and somehow they would have to get through the storm.

Neither of them had any idea that the captain had decided to stay closer to the peninsula instead of heading out into the open sea as the navigational charts had plotted. He realized he could be in trouble with his company because he was going to lose a lot more time than he already had. However, he had been in other squalls and had sailed all over the world, and something about this storm bothered him. The pressure was lower than normal, and he was very uneasy. If only the ship could have left Progresso on time. But that had not happened. It is better to be safe than sorry he thought. Being late was never a good thing, but he felt it was better than sailing directly into the tempest his satellite was indicating.

Meanwhile none of the passengers seemed concerned with the captain's report. Only Fiona felt uneasy. Just before she was ready to leave Morgan knocked to see if there was anything she needed before he went to dinner. He did not seem his usual self either.

"I have been on a lot of cruises and I think this is going to be a bad storm, Morgan. If only our bus had not broken down."

"Don't worry, Miss Fiona. We will be fine. Maybe it is better that you were late. I have sailed with this captain many times, and I trust he will do the right thing. I have always believed what is meant to happen will happen, no matter how we try to change it. We cannot control the weather, but I know our captain will take every precaution, and I have complete faith in his abilities. Now you and Mr. Devlin go enjoy your drinks and dinner, and I will have your rooms ready when you come back. You have had a challenging day, but when you two wake up tomorrow the sun will be shining just as the captain said."

Just then there was another knock on her door and when she opened it Devlin was standing there with white pants and a black shirt.

"Devlin, I don't know what it is with you and me and dressing for dinner but this is really weird."

As Devlin looked at Fiona wearing a pair of white pants and a black top, he started laughing.

"I guess we share a penchant for the same wardrobe, at least when it comes to being on shipboard."

When they entered the bar they noticed the shades had been drawn over the picture windows. After they gave their drink orders Fiona asked the waiter why the windows were covered.

"The captain said we should do this so people will not get too worried about how nasty the sea looks."

Fiona nodded as the waiter took off to get their drinks. Devlin had ordered a scotch and soda and Fiona some red wine. It was not too long before the waiter re-turned with their order.

"I don't want to talk about anything too serious right now. Why don't you tell me a little bit about your daughter?"

Devlin started to talk about Molly and the degrees she had earned as Fiona took a drink of her wine. Just then they heard a loud bang as if something had hit the ship. It was followed by several more bangs. At the same time the boat started rocking from side to side with such motion that most of the bottles behind the bar fell to the floor and broke. They could hear the glass smashing and smell the alcohol from the broken bottles. Most of the chairs had people in them, but the few empty chairs went sailing across the floor. Luckily all the tables were bolted down.

The boat continued swaying and rocking as if it were being pushed sideways. They could hear screams coming from some of the other guests as they tried to hold on to their table. Finally, Devlin stood up and carefully grabbing Fiona's hand took her behind the bar where there wasn't any broken glass. They sat down on the floor against the wall, and Devlin held her as the rocking continued.

"Please everyone sit on the floor and anchor yourself," they heard a voice saying over the loudspeaker. "We have been hit by a microburst and the seas will be very rough for a little bit longer but the worst is over."

For the next half hour they sat there as the boat continued its rough rocking. They could hear the chairs sliding across the room and the moans from some of the people who had been hit with flying debris. Devlin had his arm around her and she lay with her head on his shoulder and her eyes closed praying the rocking would soon stop.

Fiona had heard about microbursts, but with all her time at sea she had never experienced one. She knew that normally the crew could deviate from storms. But a microburst happened in a small area about two miles wide and really came out of nowhere. It could hit a ship without warning.

Finally the rocking abated. Looking down at her shirt she realized it was a good thing she had worn black. She knew she had spilled wine all over herself. There were some spots on her white pants, but the majority of it had spilled on her shirt. She was also a little sick to her stomach from the sideways rocking.

"You know, Devlin, I normally don't get seasick

from the normal up and down wave action; but this sideways motion is not doing much for my stomach."

"I am glad it is not just me feeling seasick. I did not want to embarrass myself in front of you."

Fiona smiled at Devlin's words. She was also wondering why she was worried about her clothes with all the havoc going on around them. I guess it just keeps my mind off my stomach she thought. But right now we need to check on the people who are hurt.

"Let's go see if we can help those people who seem to be in trouble."

Luckily there were no extremely serious injuries, but there was a lot of blood and a couple of people with apparent broken legs or arms. The bartender handed towels from behind the bar to all the people who weren't hurt. Fiona, Devlin and a few others tended to the people who were bleeding. There was not much they could do for the people with broken bones except hold their hands and talk to them until help came.

The ship had a plan in place for emergencies, and Fiona marveled at the efficiency as help quickly arrived. The bartender had called on the ship's phone with a report of damage and it was not long before stretchers came to take the more seriously hurt people to the hospital area. Those members of the crew who were trained in first aid came in and tended to the people who were bleeding. Everyone else was asked to go to their staterooms until the public areas could be cleaned up.

They were told an announcement would be made when they could return to the various areas for dinner. Right now the crew needed to work on helping the injured guests and cleaning up the food areas.

When they returned to their suites, Morgan was just coming off the service elevator.

"Miss Fiona. Mr. Devlin. Are you two all right?"

Fiona realized both she and Devlin had blood all over their pants, but that was from helping the injured passengers.

"We are fine, Morgan. We plan to take showers and change our clothes. Actually I think I will just throw these clothes away since I don't know if I can get the blood out."

"I am sure the ship will compensate you for your clothes."

"That is the least of my worries right now. Why don't you go and help where you are needed."

"First, I will open up a bottle of wine for the two of you. I don't suppose you had a chance to eat dinner yet? I know some of the crew got hurt and I would like to help them. I heard two dancers who were performing during the dress rehearsal when the microburst hit, fell and broke their legs."

"Morgan, don't worry about us. You need to go help where ever you can. We are fine here on our own."

"All right, Miss Fiona. I will open a bottle for each of you. Then when I have time later, after the crisis has passed, I will bring you some dinner."

Devlin nodding his head said, "Fine, Morgan. I don't think either of us is very hungry since our stomachs are a little upset. Whatever you do is fine. However, the wine is greatly appreciated. We probably should have ginger ale, but we needed a drink after what we saw this afternoon and now this. The wine is not scotch which I ordered in the bar, but it will definitely do."

Turning and looking at her Devlin said, "How about I bring my bottle over to your place in about a half hour? Does that give you enough time to get cleaned up?"

Nodding yes, Fiona opened the door of her cabin.

Morgan followed her in, and taking a bottle of Merlot from her bar, opened it and quickly left for Devlin's suite.

Another shower she was thinking as she got back under the spray. This has been quite a day. They say things happen in threes but maybe we have had enough for one day.

Fiona, like Devlin, thought they had been in the storm the captain had mentioned. They had no idea the microburst had nothing to do with the squall the crew topside was monitoring.

Meanwhile the captain was rethinking his course. He had a feeling getting over to the Cancun/Cozumel area might shelter the ship from the tempest and keep them all safer. He knew it was going to be a bad night but it was too late to get back into port and frankly the ship would do better in the open sea.

The captain had tried to reach the home office but no one was there to give him guidance. Ultimately it was his decision that would be on the line in an emergency. And it was probably a better idea to sail into Cozumel in the morning after the storm. That way they could get the injured off the ship so they could get needed medical help quicker than if he sailed directly back to Florida. But no one, except his officers, knew what the captain's new decision was.

Chapter Twenty-Six

It was not long before Devlin knocked on her door. Neither one of them had much to say to each other. They turned the TV on to a music channel and sat sipping their wine while munching on some crackers. Fiona had looked out her window, but night had descended so it was hard to see anything. The ship was rising and falling in the waves, but at least the terrible side to side rolling had stopped. Both of them could feel their stomachs getting better.

"If it is going to stay rough tonight, it is probably better we don't have a lot of food in our stomachs. I have never had a problem with sea sickness until that side rolling from the microburst, and it is better to be prepared for the bad weather that is predicted tonight. I don't want to be sick in the middle of a gale."

Laughing at him Fiona said, "but wine will not bother you like food might? I know Morgan is right. We are going to be just fine. This is turning into quite a cruise. I wish I could go to sleep right now, then it would be morning, the sun would be shining and this whole day would be over."

About an hour later Morgan brought a tray with some lasagna and breadsticks. "Sorry this is all I could get. It was in the oven, so it didn't get thrown around. I will turn your beds down now and then I need to go back and help with the injured."

"Don't worry about the beds. Just go help where you are needed. Devlin and I are very fortunate that we did not get seriously hurt. Don't bother to come back for the tray. I will rinse off and pile all the dishes in our little sink in the bar area. You can get everything in the morning."

You are not supposed to be taking care of dishes on a cruise, but since I won't come back until morning it will definitely help if you rinse them off, Miss Fiona. Thank you so much. We have some crew who are seriously hurt, and they really need my assistance."

"Is there anything we can do to help?"

"No, just knowing you are safe here in your suites greatly relieves my mind. Have a good evening and I will see both of you in the morning."

"Good night, Morgan," they said at the same time.

Neither one of them was extremely hungry so they just picked at the food. "If you don't mind, I think I will go back to my suite now. I am really emotionally drained from our day, although seeing those ruins was a real highlight of my travel writing career. I think I will turn on a movie and hopefully the television will put me to sleep."

Watching as Devlin left her suite, she gathered up the dishes and rinsed them before stacking them in the sink. Deciding going to bed early was probably a good idea; she climbed under the covers, and began reading the book she had started on the bus that afternoon. She could feel the ship moving up and down in the waves, and with the rocking motion she soon drifted off to sleep with the book still in her hands.

Fiona was having a vivid dream about being on a roller coaster as a giant snake was slithering towards her when a clap of thunder instantly awakened her. Looking at the clock by her bed, she saw it read 2:30 a.m. The movement of the boat was very unnerving. Hearing more thunder, she looked out her balcony window. Lightening could be seen all over the sky. But the scariest part was when the boat dropped down into a giant trough. The waves had to be over twenty feet high. It seemed forever before the ship rose up again. It reminded her of the movie "The Perfect Storm."

As the boat dropped into another trough, she was so frightened she knew she could not stay alone in her cabin. Going out into the hallway, she began knocking loudly on Devlin's door. Within twenty seconds his door opened and seeing him standing there calmed her fears somewhat. Just then the boat dropped into another giant trough, and she felt herself fall against him.

She heard herself say, "I am really scared. Can I come into your room with you?"

"Let's get into bed together, Fiona. I don't think it is safe standing up like this."

Too frightened for words she climbed into bed with him. He put his arm around her neck. She lay partly on top of him with her stomach pressed against his side. She put her arms around him as his other arm circled her waist. With her face pressed against his chest they both closed their eyes against the storm.

Never having been in a squall this bad she wondered if Devlin, who was new to cruising, understood the power of this gale. Opening her eyes she looked up at him. She realized immediately how frightened he also felt. They both knew their survival was at stake.

As they held each other a peace descended, because they knew they had no control over the outcome. If this was the end, at least they would not die alone. They heard an announcement from the bridge asking all the passengers in the lower cabins to slowly and carefully move up to the show lounge.

I am really glad we are already up high, Fiona thought to herself. I would hate to have to go to the show lounge. It would be uncomfortable, as well as loud and noisy, and worst of all there are no windows so you don't feel as if you could escape. She knew fleeing the fury of this storm was just an illusion, but she still did not like the idea of feeling closed in. I would rather be in bed behind a curtain she was thinking. Devlin's drape was slightly ajar; and they could see the lightening as well as hear the thunder, which totally unnerved them, yet they tried to remain calm.

As she lay pressed against Devlin she felt her body becoming aroused. She could not believe with the storm raging all around them that she could be having these kinds of feelings assaulting her. Perhaps the thought of dying or seeing the dog being eaten by the python had numbed her mind to horror that day. Or perhaps she just wanted to reaffirm that she was alive. As she looked up and gazed into Devlin's eyes she could sense he felt the pull, too. What bad timing she thought. But then again maybe it was perfect timing.

Without thinking about what they were doing he leaned towards her and their lips touched. It was a moment in which their two worlds met, and they became like one. She had refused to believe she could feel this way about a man. But now that it was happening, she knew she could not deny what she was feeling. She could not stop even if she wanted to, and she knew it was too late for Devlin to stop, too. Neither one of them wanted the moment to end.

They were both surprised by their equal passion. Neither had felt longing like this in years. Devlin was also torn. He desired her more than anything, but he still fought the idea of wanting anyone. It had been so very long since he had felt anything for a woman he wanted to jump out of the bed and run away. But it was too late for that. He touched her face with his hands, and when he heard her breath catch he knew he could no longer resist her. Neither of them had been ready for this in the past, but now it felt just right.

He heard her say "yes" as her lips once again moved closer to his, and he lost control. Hearing her moan as he passionately kissed her, he knew they both felt the tempest inside their cabin as well as out on the sea.

It had been so long since she had felt any kind of desire for a man that Fiona was stunned by the strong feelings coursing through her. Her body became more and more aroused as he pulled her even closer. She had never felt such a strong pull with Jason and was filled with wonder as she and Devlin made love.

The storm continued to rage outside, but they were no longer aware of its fury. They became totally lost in each other and when it was finally over, they were so spent, the two of them quickly fell asleep.

A little later, feeling a terrible ache in her stomach, Fiona opened her eyes and saw Devlin watching her. She smiled at him, and his lips once again descended on hers. She quickly lost the wonder of what was happening as once again Devlin made love to her in a way she had never experienced before.

When it was over, she realized the ship was no longer rocking. When Devlin pulled his curtain back they saw calm seas and the first rays from the rising sun just as the captain and Morgan had promised.

Getting back into bed Devlin once again locked her in his embrace, and as they watched the sun rise they both drifted off to sleep again.

As she awakened and saw Devlin looking at her, smiling she said, "I don't know whether to be embarrassed or not. Nothing like this has ever happened to me before."

The heat and fire of their shared passion had left them both breathless. Their eyes looked stunned by the powerful chemistry between them.

"I think the time for embarrassment ended the second time we made love. And I certainly hope it will not be our last."

Fiona blushed at Devlin's remarks, and just at that moment they heard a knock on the cabin door.
Devlin put on his robe and went to answer it. He was gone almost ten minutes, and Fiona was getting worried something had happened when he finally appeared at the bedroom door.

Sitting up she pulled at the sheets to cover herself as Devlin said, "That was just the spookiest conversation I ever had. It was Morgan in case you wondered."

Fiona nodded knowing it could not have been anyone else.

"He was very concerned when you did not answer your door, so I told him you were in here with me. I hope that was okay."

"He would have found out sooner or later anyway. With such a terrible storm I am sure he would have been worried about us and how we coped. But you were sure chatting with him a long time."

"I ordered coffee for us, but he had some strange news. Some officer friend of his told him the captain had been in touch with the main office. I guess the captain had been very worried about the storm, but did not want to alarm anyone. Knowing it would cost him a lot of time he deviated from the main course and sailed closer to the island of Cozumel instead of heading directly across the gulf. He was worried about getting the injured from the microburst medical help quickly this morning, and he thought it was more important to get the injured to proper medical facilities as soon as possible."

He continued, "Anyway his office was not angry with him even though we will be late arriving in Florida. They knew he had made the right decision. They were just happy everyone, as well as the ship, was safe even though we will be delayed getting back. We will miss our planes, but we can call our offices to have our flights changed when we dock at Cozumel. Looks like our trip will be extended by a day."

"I cannot imagine the storm being worse than what we went through, but I am glad the captain made the safer decision even if it did not feel like it last night. I know it is better to be in open water rather than docked during such a bad storm, and sailing closer to land also probably sheltered us from the worst of it."

"That is not all. It's a good thing our bus broke down yesterday. Everyone thought we would have run ahead of the storm if we left on time. But it appears the gale was faster and more fierce than previously suspected. Two cargo ships left Progresso about the time we were scheduled to leave and they followed the regularly plotted course. There has been no word from either ship! They are hoping perhaps their radios went out, but it does not looking promising."

Fiona looked at Devlin as he spoke, and she shivered with the news he had just relayed.

"That is terrible. That could have been us out there. What we went through was dreadful but at least we are alive to tell the tale."

"For all the bad luck we had yesterday it turned out to be good luck in a way. Serendipity was on our side it seems."

"I think I hear Morgan out there. I asked him to deliver coffee and Danish to your patio. I hope you don't mind."

"Not at all." Fiona was always amazed when Devlin asked her opinion. She was so used to Jason doing whatever he wanted without seeking her input, and she realized that was one reason she had never seriously looked for another man to live with. She liked knowing her opinion counted as far as Devlin was concerned.

"How about we jump into the shower together," he said with a twinkle in his eyes. "Then we can open the partition between our patios, and enjoy this beautiful calm morning before we arrive at the port."

"I don't know why, but taking a shower together is something my ex and I never did. I like these new experiences."

"Wait until I get you in there. Maybe I can come up with some even more interesting things to do in a shower."

Once again she found herself blushing, but her curiosity got the better of her.

Chapter Twenty-Seven

The shower was even more fun than Devlin had promised. Wrapping herself in a towel, Fiona went to her suite to get dressed. She did not have any shorts with her but put on a pair of pedal pushers, a white T-shirt and some flip flops.

When she walked out to the balcony, Devlin was already sitting there having a cup of coffee and reading the satellite newspaper Morgan had delivered.

"You look delicious, Fiona."

"Devlin, you cannot possibly be hungry," she said with a sparkle in her eye.

"I am starved in more ways than one. It has been an extremely long time since I have been with a woman. Besides with our light dinner and all the activity last night, I feel like I have not eaten in days."

Laughing she handed him a Danish to go with his coffee. "I also ordered scrambled eggs, pancakes, bacon and oatmeal. Morgan should be back in a little while with the rest of our breakfast."

"Here we go again eating too much."

As Fiona sat in her chair drinking some orange juice Devlin took her hand. She sighed as she looked at him and then out to sea. What a perfect place with a perfect man she thought. Could it get any better? She did not think so. Despite the storm she loved cruising. You could run into squalls anywhere you went. She was not about to stop traveling just to escape a gale. Bad weather could hit where anyone lived.

Soon they heard a knock and the butler came in, rolling a cart full of food.

Laughing as he came in she said, "I think Devlin got carried away ordering breakfast."

"It is important to keep up your strength, Miss Fiona. On a day like today, and especially after last night, it is just good to be alive."

"Amen," Devlin said.

"Do you two have any special plans today?"

"Now that we have this unscheduled stop at Cozumel we may take a taxi into town. Devlin has never been here and we can have the cab take us to the Mayan ruins on the island. They are not as spectacular as the ones we have seen, but it will help round out his education of the Mayan culture."

Continuing she added, "Then we can go sit in the plaza and watch the tourists while we have a cerveza! We will just grab lunch somewhere. I know the ship personnel will be busy getting the injured off the ship, and I heard an announcement that we are sailing at 5:00 p.m. We will definitely go to the steakhouse restaurant for dinner tonight. Could you make us a reservation for 7:30 p.m.?"

Devlin nodded his approval of what she was telling the butler.

"Yes, I will take care of your dinner reservations. Don't worry."

"Oh, and Morgan, you can go in and clean our bedrooms now. We plan to sit out here for awhile, so we will be out of your way. And then we won't need you the rest of the day. I am sure you could use some time to yourself after all the things that happened last night."

"Thank you, Miss Fiona. I could use a little down

time today."

As the butler left to clean their cabins Devlin said, "I think it will be very difficult when I do not have a butler to see to my every need on my next cruise. It certainly does not take long to get spoiled."

"I was thinking the same thing. But right now it just feels good to be sitting here with you and thinking about going into town with nothing more to do than seeing some ruins, having a beer, and watching the world go by. Tomorrow we can fire up our computers, and get some thoughts down while they are fresh in our minds.

These suites are wonderful, and it is great to have a butler. But we need to pay the piper. We also need to call our offices when we get to town and have them rebook our flights. We will be at sea all day tomorrow so probably the evening of the next day will be our best option."

"We get an extra day in paradise, Devlin! As the saying goes, 'This is a tough job, but someone has to do it; and I can't wait to get busy doing nothing."

After eating breakfast they decided they would definitely not do lunch on the ship and just go directly to town. The pier the ship docked at was a distance from the downtown area. They had seen the injured being taken off the vessel as they were eating breakfast and knew the hectic disembarking pace had settled down.

"Most of the passengers have probably disembarked for the day and I'll bet the gangway is not crowded now."

"Nodding at him she said, "Let's go find a taxi to take us to the ruins. When we get back to town we can sit in the main plaza and have some snacks with our Coronas."

"Then perhaps we could come back to the ship and have time for a nap before dinner," he said with a glint in his eyes.

"You are insatiable. But keep it up. I would never

have guessed I could enjoy 'sleeping' so much. Now I know how Bryan and Diana felt on our last cruise."

They made their way down the gangplank and skipped having their photo taken. They both found phones to call their offices and let them know what had happened. As they exited the terminal building Devlin saw a man holding a sign advertising a price to the ruins.

"I do a nice city tour and ride to the ruins, sir. Then I can drop you off downtown in the main plaza for shopping or bring you back to the ship. The cost will be $40.00 for the tour."

Looking at Fiona as she nodded at him, Devlin quickly agreed to the set price. They both thought it was a fair charge and followed the taxi driver to his car for the ride to the ruins.

"That is $20.00 each, and we can give him $5.00 extra as a tip if he does a good job."

Settling next to each other in the back seat of the taxi, the two of them listened as the driver told them about the island. Fiona had been to Cozumel several times, but she sat quietly thinking maybe she would learn something new for a future article.

Immediately beginning his tour the cabbie said, "Cozumel is twenty-nine miles long and about nine miles wide. The population is right around 65,000. What everyone seems to love here is the small town atmosphere. We do not allow development as you find on the mainland. In fact the interior of the island is now protected to eliminate further growth. However we are very prosperous, and due to tourism everyone here has a job. It is not unusual to see five to seven cruise ships docked daily during the winter months. They sail away by 5:00 p.m., and we become a sleepy little town again. Even the prices in the stores go down, I am sorry to say."

The cab driver continued, " We are twelve miles from the coast but what causes my island to be so famous is a series of coral reefs that makes this tropical paradise one of the top diving destinations in the world. We have a high speed ferry to take people from the island to Playa del Carmen on the mainland. It's about a forty-five minute ride. What you might not realize is that the channel is about three thousand feet deep. That side of the island has calm waters and sandy shores. Naturally the ruins are located there. The eastern side which we will drive later is much rockier since it faces the open sea. It is not protected as it is on the west. You will notice the pounding surf that hides powerful undertows."

So far Fiona had not heard anything she did not already know; and wondered, since the scattered Mayan ruins had not been well preserved, if they were worth seeing. She had read about the pirates and smugglers who used the protected coves for their hideouts. After World War II servicemen who had been stationed on the island returned for vacations. But it was in the early 1960's, when Jacques Cousteau made a television documentary, that Cozumel gained worldwide prestige as a top diving spot.

The land was flat, and the interior was pure jungle with many insects. Since the interior had never been developed it seemed rather desolate. It was the beaches that made the island inviting to the many tourists who visited.

Devlin had his arm around her. She rested her head against his shoulder, and as they watched the sea as they headed out of the downtown area. They had glimpsed the budget hotels, shops, restaurants, and nightspots in the only town on the island, San Miguel. Fiona had pointed out the Plaza del Sol, the central plaza, to Devlin as the taxi had scooted through town.

She noticed the cab driver nodding his head in

agreement as she told Devlin how pretty the plaza was in the spring when poinciana trees were covered with orange blossoms.

"There is a statue of Benito Juarez, a former Mexican president and hero, in the plaza, and it is fun to sit there and watch the world go by as you drink your cerveza."

"Maybe we will get a chance to come back here sometime in the spring."

This whole experience was so new to Fiona. As she looked at Devlin she wondered if their liaison was meant to last. She still did not know if she was looking for a long term relationship. She knew that everyone is on a different path.

People's journeys may intersect one day but then go in a different direction the next. As much as she liked Devlin, she would not take it personally if things did not work out between them. She had to admit she was still bothered by their age difference, although he did not seem to mind.

The San Gervasio ruins had never been preserved as other Mayan sites on the mainland. Miguel, their cab driver, began telling them about the Mayan on Cozumel.

"Cozumel was the equivalent of Mecca to the Mayans. Sometime during their lifetime the Mayan people would make a journey to this island. The site you are about to see has not been well preserved. However you can still see faint traces of paint on the first structure we come to. These were the first ruins discovered by the Spanish. However, Hurricane Wilma was unkind to this area. It was a Category 5 storm and was very vicious. But at the same time, something wonderful did come from that hurricane. The storm uncovered some ruins that are just as magnificent as Tulum. They are called El Ramonal and the government is working on preserving the site. They should open in another three to four years and will become a very important Mayan site right here on Cozumel."

Neither Fiona nor Devlin had heard anything about this site. She wrote down the name the cab driver had given her, so she could do some further research on these recently discovered ruins.

As they entered the parking lot the first thing they saw was the typical mixture of Mexican crafts, jewelry, and T-shirt shops. They passed through the shopping area, and continued through the admission area. Then a guide took them around the ruins. He explained that Cozumel had been purchased by a single family for five dollars in gold one hundred fifty years ago. When the family had died out, the land had been donated back to the island.

The ruins of San Gervasio were in various states of decline but one could still see the columns and outlines of the buildings. The most fascinating site was an arch which was also a calendar. Leading up to the arch were uneven white rocks which were actually a road that ran for three miles to the sea. The guide showed them a picture from an archaeological book that theorized that the arch was not only a gateway into the ancient city but was once actually a pyramid shaped structure that the Mayans were known to build.

Although the site was not as awesome as the ruins Fiona had seen on the mainland, she was still impressed by what they were seeing and was happy they had the opportunity to stop in Cozumel and view them. She had stopped at this island previously but had never bothered to visit the ruins.

As they returned to the taxi several birds flew by them. The cabbie asked if the guide had told them about the swallows.

Shaking their heads "no," Miguel explained. "The ceremonial center you just visited was dedicated to the love and fertility goddess, Ixchel. When temples were dedicated to her; she sent her favorite bird, the swallow, in gratitude. That was how our island got its name since 'Cuzamel' meant "Land of the Swallows."

Before they knew it they were being dropped back in town. Miguel said he would be back in an hour to pick them up and take them back to the ship. Normally he would not have come back for them since there were plenty of taxis around. However he didn't have any more work for the day and he thought they would appreciate his gesture with a nice tip.

Neither of them was interested in shopping. There was a bar on the corner that faced both the main street and the plaza. They ordered Coronas with chips and salsa and sat watching the people as they strolled by. It was very relaxing sitting there despite the circumstances of being where they were. Fiona thought it had been a perfect day as well as enlightening.

As their eyes met, Fiona felt a deep longing in her stomach. I have not felt this way about someone from the opposite sex since I was in high school she was thinking. I have to quit worrying about our ages and what might or might not happen. Yesterday is over, and tomorrow is yet to come. I need to live now in the moment.

I have a couple of friends who are always chasing some dream that is over the next hill. Living seems to pass them by as they chase the future. I don't want the years to pass me by as I wait for some unknown future happiness. Life is a gift given to us. That is why they call it the present.

With mother gone I realize how short our journey through life can be. I have sometimes wondered if I could ever meet a man to love the way my mother and father loved each other. They really had something special and I was always a little envious of their relationship. But at the same time, it makes me realize that a strong, happy bond between two people is possible.

While Fiona was reflecting on her current circumstances; Devlin was also thinking about this new relationship between the two of them. After losing someone he loved so much and being alone these last few years, he never imagined in his wildest dreams he would feel so intense about someone again. It seemed fate had a way of changing things.

He kept thinking about what might have happened if their bus had not broken down and they had left port on time or if Fiona had not been on this ship with him. There are so many "ifs", and yet things seemed to have worked out the way they were meant to. He knew he was attracted to her, but he didn't think he would have acted on those desires if she had not knocked on his door last night. To have found this magic of love again seemed almost unbelievable.

It was at that point in his musings that they both heard the horn as the taxi pulled up. It was time to go back to the ship and see where this new journey would lead them.

Chapter Twenty-Eight

When they returned to the ship they found the wall between their two suites pushed opened.

"I guess there is no use pretending to Morgan that we are not having a relationship."

Devlin nodded as he took her hand and led her into his bedroom. As he undressed her, his eyes never left her drawing them closer together. A moment that took their breaths away passed between them surprising both with the sexual implications.

I cannot believe I am feeling like this at my age Fiona thought. The connection they were feeling was so intense they could not refuse to acknowledge it. They both wanted to touch each other and began taking the other's clothes off.

Devlin closed the small space that remained between them and as their lips met he could smell her scent as he gently laid her down on the bed. Soon they were so lost in each other the outside world ceased to exist. Afterwards they snuggled close and once again drifted off to sleep.

They were awakened by someone knocking on their door, and Fiona noticed it was dark outside. It was 6:30 p.m. and night had fallen. Devlin got up to answer the door realizing it was probably Morgan checking in.

As he came back into the bedroom, Fiona realized she had been right in her assumption.

"That was Morgan, and he wanted to know if we wanted anything. I told him we would be dressing for dinner; and if he would come back after we left around 7:30 p.m., he could clean the rooms, and we would not need anything else until morning. I thought he was probably tired after all the help he gave to the injured last night."

"All the crew on board works so hard. It is good that we can give Morgan a little extra time to himself. And now I want to jump in the hot tub and soak awhile. My muscles are a little sore from the work out they have taken. I guess I have you to thank for that."

Her eyes sparkled as she left Devlin's bedroom for her own to find her swimsuit. As she was sinking into the tub, Devlin came out of the deck with two glasses of wine in each hand. He was not wearing a swimsuit.

"I cannot believe how decadent I feel soaking in this tub and drinking wine with you."

"You are right about that. But I thought perhaps you might get into the tub without a swimsuit," he said as his eyebrow rose in amusement.

"I guess it was a little silly after what we have been doing. I've never gotten into a hot tub without a suit before so it seemed natural to wear one."

She snuggled up next to him, and they drank their wine and watched the sun set. The ship had sailed right at 5:00 p.m., and it felt a little bittersweet knowing they were leaving paradise and would soon be back in the real world. Before they departed for the ruins they had called their offices, and they knew their new travel arrangements home were being taken care of.

When they got to Miami they would be leaving approximately the same time, but would be taking separate flights home. Devlin was flying to Chicago O'Hare while Fiona would be flying to Milwaukee, Wisconsin. They knew it would soon be time to talk about any supposed future they might have, but for the present it was nice just sitting together without a care in the world.

Reluctantly they got out of the tub after about a half hour. They wanted to shower off the chemicals before dressing for dinner.

"I know we don't have time for fooling around, but I sure would like it if you would join me in the shower."

Smiling at him she nodded her head. She still found it amazing how naturally they had come together as a couple. She and her ex had never shared this type of closeness. Actually as she thought back to her marriage, she realized the only thing Jason had ever been truly intimate with had been the bottle!

Not wishing him ill, she hoped that perhaps he and Vicky had a better relationship than the two of them had shared together. Knowing what he had done to her, still hurt. But since there was nothing she could change about having no children, she had tried to let any negative feelings towards her ex go. She was happy and content with her life and that was all that mattered.

Chapter Twenty-Nine

As promised the shower was fun, and then they had a relaxing dinner together. Fiona could not believe how much they had been through in the last twenty-four hours. But as they were eating, she was debating about saying something about their future together. Maybe this was just a quick shipboard fling. She had never done anything like this before, but after reflecting on what had occurred she knew she would never regret what had happened between them.

Experiencing things with Devlin that were totally new to her made her realize her mother had been right. She should never have shut herself off to the possibility of romance. She had always thought that any relations with men would be similar to what she had experienced with Jason. And life with Jason had been so boring she knew she would be happier living her life alone than going through that type of relationship again.

Even if there was no future with Devlin, although she was not promiscuous by nature and did not intend to be in the future, she would not shut herself off as she had. She had been judging all men as if they were like her ex. Now she knew how wrong she had been. Her father had always been a very thoughtful and caring husband. Life was too short, and she needed to open herself up and be prepared for a satisfying connection with someone.

As she was musing over how the relationship with Devlin might develop, he was also thinking about the same thing. He could not believe how quickly and comfortably the bond between them had formed. He was not sure what would happen, but he knew she was one of the better things that had happened to him in his lifetime. He still did not know if he could give himself completely to someone as he had with Shannon. Although the ache had dulled, he remembered how painful his life had felt for so long after she died. He did not know if he could survive the hurt of another loss like that.

For now he needed to put those thoughts aside. Their relationship was so fresh and fun, and it had been a long time since he had felt this happy. He did not want to lose those feelings right now. He knew Fiona had similar commitment issues. Drifting into an affair was probably what they both needed at this point in time. They could worry about what might happen later. He felt so much better coming to this conclusion. Tomorrow he would broach the subject of their tentative future. Right now it was time to enjoy.

"How do you feel about going dancing after dinner?"

"That sounds like fun. I feel bad thinking about all the people who had to leave the ship in Cozumel because of getting hurt, and here we are so happy. It doesn't seem quite right. Yet I have been alone for so many years, especially after mother died. Which reminds me, I wonder how Miriam is coping with her mother's apparent death?"

"From the little I saw I don't think she is too concerned. Sometimes she seems like a different person. It is almost as if she were shouting to the world, 'Good riddance to bad rubbish. If you know what I mean."

"Her mother was so trying. I don't know how she lived with that pressure for so long. A normal person probably would have cracked."

"Well she sure seemed to be enjoying herself when I saw her with her 'boy toy." And she was dressed so differently from those prom-like dresses Emma wore on the ship. She must have been doing some serious shopping in Miami."

"Devlin, how did you know those were prom dresses? I would never have guessed you knew anything about fashion," she asked teasingly.

"Actually I don't know much about fashion. Peter and Brody were talking about the dresses Miriam and her mother wore at dinner each night. They called Emma's outfits a perfect example of prom dresses from the sixties. And I thought they had a point. I wonder if she will still be in Miami when we get back there?"

"I doubt we will have time to find out and frankly I could care less."

That statement was rather ironic because at that very moment Maxine was thinking fondly of Fiona, and how she seemed to really care about her.

There were a couple of nights when she had awakened with nightmares that Emma was still alive and berating her for throwing her over the balcony. Even though Miriam could not remember anything that happened that evening, Maxine felt she had gotten away with the murder, and knew she would have no regrets for what she had done.

However, she had a bit of a scare the day before when she thought she saw her mother walking down the street right in front of her. It was foolish of her to think Emma had somehow survived going overboard. It seemed the woman could not leave her alone even in death. Oh well all will be forgotten when I get my hands on Emma's money, she thought.

Zack had asked her about the tragedy and what had happened when they first met. He told her he did not want to upset her, but it was hard not to bring it up when he had read about it in the newspapers. It might have looked strange if he had not mentioned it. She had tears in her eyes as she told him she tried to block the thought from her mind. In her opinion if her mother had truly fallen overboard, and it looked as if that was the case, she could not imagine how awful that would have been for Emma. She refused to say anything else and Zack had dropped the subject.

Having no idea the man was an insurance investigator, and one of the best in the business, she dismissed his questions as curiosity. She thought he was a gigolo who picked up wealthy older women to party with. Not that she was wealthy…yet. But she was definitely working towards that goal.

Wondering how long it would take the insurance company to pay her off now occupied her mind. Even without a body, it was obvious that Emma had not been anywhere on the ship and must have drowned. And if they suspected her, she reasoned they would have kept questioning her. So for now she felt she was in the clear. All she wanted was to continue dancing each night away with Zack.

Meanwhile sailing in the Caribbean, Fiona and Devlin were also dancing the night away never guessing what was going on in Miriam's life.

Chapter Thirty

Fiona awoke the next morning feeling a little depressed. It had been so much fun with Devlin the evening before, and sleeping with him was so comfortable. She knew she was going to miss him when she went home.

As they sat on her balcony having breakfast, Devlin brought up the subject of "them" first.

"I know you must feel as I do that everything has happened very fast."

She started to interrupt him; but he said, "No, let me continue. We have so little time left together. I think this liaison has taken us both by surprise especially since neither one of us was expecting anything to happen. I know it is too early to know what will develop. We do live a distance from each other, but I would like to continue this relationship when we get home if you would."

"I would like that, too. We are getting into the holiday season, but maybe we could get together for weekends. I think we only live about an hour and a half apart. If we take things slowly, we will get a chance to know each other better. I do not think either one of us is ready for any long term commitment, but I also don't want to see this end after we leave the ship."

"Fiona, I think it is only fair to tell you about Shannon. We were very much in love, and we were going to be married. Then she needed brain surgery, and she did not come out of the operating room alive. I have had a hard time getting over the pain of losing her. I have been so afraid to take a chance on a meaningful relationship and have never really been serious with anyone since Shannon died. I know you wondered why I was so short with you that day we met. It is just that when you looked up at me, you had the same color eyes as Shannon's, and it took me by surprise. You don't look anything like her, but your eye color brought the pain back for an instant and I snapped at you."

"I am glad you told me about her. I also have issues. My husband was an alcoholic and emotionally controlling. He had a vasectomy and never told me, so that is why we never had children. Actually he did not tell me about his surgery until we were divorcing. I guess to say I have issues with trusting someone is putting it mildly. I have enjoyed my freedom and am not sure about committing to anyone either. So I guess we are both broken in some way."

"Why don't we just let things develop in their own fashion, and see how it all plays out?"

"I think that is an excellent suggestion."

Fiona was glad Devlin had brought up their possible future. She was finding it difficult to think about anything except him. Knowing she would not have to give him up after they had just found each other, made their all too soon separation bearable. She could feel the tension release from his body after he told her about Shannon.

Realizing a possible future together was a precarious situation, they both wanted to try and see where their relationship might go. Even if things did not work out for now they were willing to make an effort towards being together. Since they both seemed to have commitment issues, at least it was a start.

Their last day at sea was fun and neither of them was looking forward to the end of this cruise.

"I don't know if we will ever get a chance to stay in a suite like this again, but it sure has made for an interesting journey. I am debating about writing of this experience. Do you think the average cruiser would even care to know these suites exist?"

"I think you have a point. You need to have a lot of money to stay in these rooms, and they are definitely out of reach for the average tourist. Most likely only one to two percent of cruisers would even consider suites like these."

"Perhaps we should just enjoy our last day at sea and not worry about work. We will have plenty of time for writing when we get home. With Thanksgiving coming and then Christmas work will definitely slow down."

"I know my editor wants at least one article done before Christmas so he can print it in our January edition. Winter and spring are big cruise seasons, and the point of these free trips is to get travelers interested in sailing as their choice of vacation."

"Do you have plans for Thanksgiving, Devlin?"

"Yes, Molly has invited me to her in-laws for dinner that day, and then the day after Thanksgiving we always go to downtown Chicago to look at the store windows and visit one of the museums. How about I plan to visit you next weekend in Wisconsin? It is still a week before Thanksgiving, and I know it will be too difficult to get away for the holiday weekend."

"That sounds perfect. I also have plans with my friend Kathy and her family."

"I do not want to hurt your feelings, but I would rather my daughter not know about you yet. I am not sure how I feel about 'us', and where our relationship is headed so I prefer Molly not knowing I am seeing someone right now. It seems like we sailed into rough seas, and it caused us to change the course of our lives. But for now a little caution is in order."

"I agree with you. Besides I can use the Thanksgiving weekend to get caught up with my research and writing. I know my boss has a trip overseas planned for me sometime the first part of next year, and I want to wrap up these Caribbean cruise articles before starting the new job."

"We really have not thoroughly explored this ship. Let's walk down to Deck 4 and then circle each floor. That way we can see the layout first hand and not have to rely on the little cheat sheet booklet the ship prints out."

"That sounds like a great idea. I don't really need the exercise after the work-out you have been putting me through, but it always feels good to get out and about."

The two of them walked down to the 4th floor and started exploring. They browsed through the shops but discovered it was all the same old stuff all the ships carried. They had a hard time getting through the shops area because the stores were having sales and had tables placed outside in the hallways. Naturally these areas were being mobbed by the cruisers looking for that final deal.

Fiona saw two of the couples she had ridden to the ship with and was happy they had not been hurt. They were looking for bargains to take home and after saying hello to her they continued their hunt.

When they reached the buffet deck, the music was blaring and everyone seemed to be drinking and eating at the barbecue taking place by the pool area. Fiona and Devlin went inside and got salads and took them aft. It was quieter out there with only the sun worshipers sitting around the adult pool. They watched the ship's wake as they ate their salads. After finishing they returned to their suites for an afternoon "nap."

Later they spent time in the hot tub, and the day passed all too quickly. Before they knew it dinner time had arrived. They skipped the show after their meal. They just wanted to be alone and snuggled up in bed together. They talked for quite awhile, but then both fell asleep. Before they knew it the morning had arrived, and Morgan was knocking on their door.

The ship had docked! Disembarking the passengers would not take as long as it normally did since the ship had not been full to capacity, and so many had been taken off at Cozumel. There was a sadness that the cruise was over.

Fiona and Devlin were both depressed, and it seemed they could not touch each other enough. It had been a very poignant time for them. For the last few days they had been living in a world of unreality, and it had been good for both of them. Now they were back in the real world. Would they discover that this interlude had only been a short affair, or would this be a relationship that would lead to a lasting commitment? Only time would tell.

They both said their good-byes to Morgan and gave him generous tips for his service. They were unhappy to be leaving knowing they would probably never see him again. After the intense time they had spent on board, he seemed more than just a butler to them.

After they left the ship they had quite a bit of time before their flights. They decided to see if they could contact Miriam. Although she was still listed at the same hotel as before, they rang her room several times to no avail.

She had gone through a very traumatic situation, and they both wished her the best as they made their way by taxi to the airport and their previous lives.

Chapter Thirty-One

The flight home had been uneventful. It was late Sunday night when Fiona's plane landed at Mitchell Field. And, oh, was it cold especially after spending so much time in the warmer climates. True to his word Devlin showed up late Friday afternoon.

It was almost as if they had not seen the other for months they were so insatiable for each other. Fiona had told Kathy she was busy over the weekend but would spend time with her on Thanksgiving Day. Kathy had not asked what she would be doing. She figured Fiona would lock herself up and write which is what she had done previously when returning from an assignment. She had no idea there was a man who would be taking up Fiona's time.

And did he ever take up her time. By the time they got out of bed it was too late to go and eat, so Fiona made them omelets instead. The next day was no better. They did not leave her condo all weekend, and the second night they had pizza delivered. Before they knew it Sunday afternoon had arrived, and Devlin had to leave. He had wanted to stay until Monday morning, but he had an appointment with his editor and had to get back.

"I am going to miss you, Fiona. Two weeks seems like such a long time to be apart."

"I am sorry we did not get a chance to walk on the

beach. I know it is cold, but it is always refreshing and does not seem bad if you bundle up. But I guess I got enough exercise this weekend."

"Why don't you take the train when you come to my condo in two weeks? If you come early on Friday I can meet you at the station and we can go have a late lunch before going back to my place. Maybe we can stay out of bed long enough to go down to the city on that Saturday."

"That would be fun. I can do some of my Christmas shopping while there. Maybe we could even take in a play."

"You don't think I will keep you too busy for a play," he asked with a twinkle in his eyes.

As it turned out Thanksgiving with their friends and family was nice, but they both missed each other so much neither one of them got much work done that weekend. They spent a lot of time talking by phone.

The following weekend Fiona took the train to Evanston, and they went to the city. They saw a matinee, but after they got back to Devlin's place they never left until Monday at noon when Fiona took the train back to Wisconsin.

They alternated weekends at each other's places, but like Thanksgiving they spent Christmas apart with their friends and family.

New Year's was a different story. By that time they were both sick of the cold weather and wanted to get away. They had caught up with their articles and were foot loose and fancy free for the moment. They had managed to keep their affair secret although there was no reason to. Now they were ready to go out in public and have fun without worrying about someone recognizing them; although Fiona did not know why that mattered. They were two single consenting adults.

Fiona didn't really care if the world knew. But Devlin was insistent on Molly not knowing. Several times she had been ready to tell Kathy what was going on, but she worried that if things ended between them, she did not want her friend to know she had failed with this new relationship.

"Why don't we go to Miami for New Year's Eve? No one knows us, and it will be fun going to those clubs. Maybe we will even run into Miriam if she is still there."

"That is a great idea, Fiona. Let's look at flights to Florida. We may want to spend a few days there so we don't get caught in the high priced holiday air rates."

"Perhaps we could rent a car and go down to the Keys for a few days. It would be enjoyable to stay a couple of nights in Key West. We hardly knew each other the last time we were there."

"Now that you don't have to go overseas until the end of February we should spend some quality time together, and it might as well be some place warm."

"I have been keeping in touch with Diana. I hope you don't mind, but I told her we were seeing each other. She seemed really excited for us. I guess when you are so happy in love you want the whole world to feel the same way. Anyway she wondered if we could come out and visit her and Bryan for a week before Valentine's Day. I told her I needed to check with you, but that it would probably be fine."

And so two days after Christmas the two of them were on their way back to Miami. They checked on Miriam when they got back to town, but discovered she had left a couple of weeks previously. Fiona had tried emailing her but had never heard anything back.

They spent New Year's Eve "clubbing." It was fun to do once but it was not a lifestyle either of them was into. They enjoyed their time much more in the laid back atmosphere of Key West. They watched the sunset and drank margaritas every night just as they had when they had been there with the ship.

All too soon it was time to leave Florida and go back to their cold northern homes. The only thing that had marred their time together was when Fiona brought up the fact that Devlin should tell his daughter about her. She was so happy she wanted to shout it out to the world. But Devlin had an irrational fear that if he told anyone about her, including his daughter, their relationship might end.

There were less than four weeks before they would be going to San Francisco. Devlin had not mentioned to Fiona that he had been emailing Bryan. If they lived closer, he knew the four of them would have been good friends. He, like Fiona, was looking forward to their California visit.

Meanwhile they continued to alternate weekends and time passed quickly. Fiona's editor had told her she would be doing a Mediterranean cruise February 23rd, and she needed to fly out on the 21st. She knew she would miss Devlin, but this assignment had been in the works for quite awhile. She had been doing some preliminary research for her trip. She did not want to worry about work while they were visiting their friends in San Francisco.

Devlin had been given an assignment to South America. It would be summer there, and he was scheduled to be gone for three weeks. It was going to be a long separation, and they wondered if it would affect their relationship. They had no idea fate would intervene in a different way before that.

Chapter Thirty-Two

"Miriam, Miriam."

"Mother, what are you doing here? You are supposed to be dead. Go away and quit bothering me."

"Miriam, I need you. Please come to me."

"Mother, you are on your own now. I finally got rid of you. You need to go away and leave me alone."

At that moment Maxine woke up realizing she was dreaming again about Emma. Why couldn't that woman just die and leave her in peace like everyone else who left this world? She was finally living her life the way she wanted to and was happy for the first time since Miriam's Randy had died.

Maxine had become stronger and stronger since Emma's demise and Miriam's personality had not been able to come out for weeks. Maxine, of course, knew about Miriam but the opposite was not true.

Maxine did not know too much about psychology but she had read about split personalities on the internet. The politically correct term was dissociative identity disorder. All she really wanted to know was if she could keep Miriam locked in forever. She loved the person she had become.

She had read that the only way Miriam could get rid of her was through treatment. Maxine knew she would never allow Miriam to do that. Besides, the woman knew nothing about her.

Sometimes Miriam would awaken and be very confused when she saw Maxine's clothes lying on the floor in her bedroom. Maxine would leave her clothes on the floor purposely because it delighted her to know how confused Miriam would be by her actions. Whenever Miriam saw the clothes she would get a migraine and ended up hanging everything back in the closet and forgetting about them.

Maxine much preferred her life to the mousy Miriam's. And since she had met Zack, her life was even better. He was perfect for her and she just hoped he felt something for her, too.

Knowing he was a gigolo was not a bother as long as he liked being around her, and they could have fun together. She had left Zack back in Miami in early December, but he had promised to join her in Los Angeles for New Year's. Meanwhile she had recently arrived home to her mother's condo. She needed to get rid of this place. It belonged to Emma. She not only refused to think of her as her mother, but wanted no reminder of the woman in any way.

Her life had begun a couple of months after Randy had died. Miriam had locked herself up in her room for weeks after the tragedy. One night Maxine found herself in a bar drinking with some men. She was in Miriam's body, but she knew she was not Miriam. That was the beginning of her secret life. She had clothes she loved that did not look at all like the ones Emma insisted Miriam wear. She kept them hidden in the back of the bedroom closet. She also knew her personality was much more forceful and assertive than "the mouse" as she referred to her other self.

She had spent a month in Miami after Emma's death. Even though she was living it up and partying every night, she hoped it looked to the cruise owners that she was awaiting news of her mother. Actually she knew there would be no news, but going back to California too soon might look bad if she started getting rid of Emma's possessions too fast. So it had been more fun to stay in Florida.

When she did return to Los Angeles, the first thing she did was arrange for the Salvation Army to come and take all the clothes belonging to both Miriam and Emma out of the condo. Except for a couple of business suits she had always liked, she got rid of everything. There were remembrances of Emma everywhere, and she wanted to eradicate them. She had called an appraiser to come and give her a price on all the paintings and furnishings. He had been very fair and had promised to come and take everything out of the building by the end of the week.

Next she had called a realtor that a friend had recommended. Acting distraught she had signed all the papers to get the condo on the market. The woman had told her it should sell quickly because it was in such a desirable location. In addition, Maxine had taken several thousand off the list price for a quick sale. An empty condo would also look more enticing. It would give prospective buyers an idea what their own belongings would look like in the place.

Feeling much better about the direction of her life, she knew she had to relocate quickly. Moving to an extended stay residence seemed the perfect answer. She had been having dreams of Emma calling to her every night since she had returned to Los Angeles. Memories of Emma's emotional abuse of Miriam haunted her constantly. Getting out of the condo should solve that problem. Then as soon as Zack returned her life of fun times would begin again.

Yes, things were definitely looking up. Once she got rid of that woman's belongings, she would be rid of Emma once and for all. At least that was the plan. For now she had gone to lunch a few times with some of Emma's closest friends. She had been grief-stricken around them, and they had felt very sorry for her.

They had always thought Emma was lucky to have such a devoted daughter. She had kept a few knick knacks and had given one to each of her mother's friends in memory of Emma. This made all of them even surer of her devotion as a daughter.

If only they knew, she thought. When she told them the memories were too much for her to bear, they all understood her putting the condo on the market. They had no idea she only wanted the money. In their eyes Miriam could do no wrong. When an insurance investigator had discretely questioned the women, they were adamant in their defense of her.

Starting tomorrow Maxine was moving to an upscale extended stay hotel with furnished one bedroom apartments. She was only going to sleep in this condo one more night. Emma would never again be able to harass her after she left this place.

A new way of life was beckoning.

Chapter Thirty-Three

January seemed to fly by. The couple continued to alternate weekends at each other's home. Fiona had talked to Devlin about meeting her friends, Kathy and Eric, and he had been agreeable. Although they still enjoyed all their "inside" time, they were also getting out and about more in their respective areas.

Kathy was excited for her friend. She was so happy Fiona had finally met a man she could love and trust. Although she had tolerated Jason for her friend's sake, she hated the way Jason would constantly find ways to put Fiona down.

From what she had observed so far the opposite was true of Devlin. He was always doing little things to make Fiona happy. And the way they laughed together Kathy had the feeling the two of them were living on a separate planet from the rest of the world. There were a lot of good men out there, and her friend was thrilled Fiona had found one. She deserved to live a life filled with happiness.

Kathy thanked God everyday that she had found true love on her first try. With the spiraling divorce rate that was obviously not always the case. She and Eric had their ups and downs. It took a lot of effort to have a committed relationship, but she knew if you worked at your marriage and nourished it things would flourish into something that would give both of you great happiness your whole life.

Knowing how important it was to respect each other was a lesson she had learned early in her marriage. You might not always agree with the other person's opinions but if you could find a way to compromise and talk about how you felt, life ran more smoothly. Her mother had told her, "Never go to bed angry with your spouse."

That seemed like a given but there have been times when it was very hard to do. However she and Eric had an early lesson in anger. A couple who had been school mates with them had married right out of high school and had a baby almost immediately. Fred had gone from one low paying job to another and would often erupt in anger around everyone.

He was never physically abusive, but the emotional outbursts kept everyone away from him. And, most of the time his anger was for totally irrational reasons. He was so stressed by his job situation and the cost of raising a family he would lash out at his wife as well as others. He did not know how to calmly express his feelings or how to express rationally what he felt emotionally.

His exploding in anger served no constructive purpose except to let off steam. He was so righteous in his opinions no one could get through to him. Kathy knew it was healthy to express your feelings when done with the right words. But Fred's outbursts never made him feel better.

Julia, his wife, had gone back to school and gotten a degree in the medical field. She became an X-Ray technician and loved it. And the money was good. She had tried to talk Fred into going to school as she had, but he flatly refused.

One summer when he was twenty-two years old he had gotten a job in construction. The money was finally what he felt he deserved, and Julia felt that perhaps their life would finally turn around. But another employee accidentally hit Fred's truck as he drove into the construction site one morning. As he exited the vehicle his temper got the better of him. Before the other man could even talk to him or reason with him, he began yelling and screaming. In the midst of his tirade he suddenly fell to the ground. The paramedics pronounced him dead at the scene!

The autopsy showed he had suffered a massive stroke. Who would have guessed that could happen to someone so young.

It was not long after that Kathy read a quote from Buddha. "Holding onto anger is like grasping a hot coal with the intent of throwing it at someone. Instead you are the only one who gets burned." That was certainly the case with Fred.

Both she and Eric were shocked when mortality hit them so early in their lives. Because of Fred, they started talking things over even more than previously and decided to try and rationally discuss their issues as they developed. They also never went to bed angry as her mother had suggested.

In a way it was sad because they had a much stronger marriage after Fred and Julia lost theirs. But Julia had eventually found peace. She met a medical technician where she worked about three years after Fred's death and fell deeply in love. She, too, had learned the importance of communicating with your spouse and had gone on to have a happy life. Once she made peace with the past her future became brighter than ever.

Meanwhile on the Saturday nights Fiona and Devlin spent in Wisconsin, the two couples went to a favorite restaurant for dinner and dancing. The two men were becoming friends, and Devlin loved it. He had traveled so much all his career he had never had a chance to forge many relationships with men.

When he was in college he had done a lot of sailing and had always liked living so close to Lake Michigan. Eric told him all about his cabin cruiser and as they talked about different engines and boats Kathy and Fiona would roll their eyes at each other. Devlin was looking forward to spending time on the boat the following summer.

The only thing that marred their happiness was his refusal to let her meet his daughter. She did not understand why he was so adamant against it.

"It's as if you are embarrassed to introduce me to her," Fiona said as she was putting her coat on to go home.

"That is not a fair thing to say."

"Well maybe not. But Devlin, I have never made any demands on you. It is almost as if you feel if I meet her, you will have to be committed to me. You know that is not true. Your ex has a husband. Why can't you have a girlfriend?"

"Let's not talk about this right now. You have to leave and I don't want you to go home angry."

"I will let it go for now, but not talking about it is not going to solve the issue. When you come to see me, you stay until Monday morning. Now, next week you have to be back by noon on Sunday because of some party that Molly is having. We see so little of each other as it is. It almost feels like we have to steal moments to be together."

"Look, Fiona. Molly does not know about you so obviously I don't want to show up to a family gathering with you in tow."

"If Molly knew about me, I could come down here next weekend and go to the party with you. Then we would have a long weekend together. As it is, because of your meeting at work you can't get to my place until later on Friday night, and then you are leaving early Sunday morning."

"I do want you to meet my daughter, and I want the two of you to get to know each other. I know you will like her, and she will like you. It just isn't going to happen next weekend. But I promise as soon as we come back from San Francisco I will introduce you."

"But we have our trips when we come back from San Francisco."

"There will be time, Fiona. I promise."

"I don't want to be a nag. It's just I enjoy your company so much and miss you when we are not together during the week."

"I know, love."

But Devlin really was not all that sure. After she left to go home he started thinking about things. Lately his stomach was tied in knots a lot. When he was with Fiona everything seemed so perfect and simple. However he knew he was falling hard for her, and it scared him to death. He wanted to be with her but he was also afraid of the emotional relationship.

He had not been tied down to anyone for ten years, and he liked his life. He never had to account for his time or consider anyone else in his plans. It had been such a long time since he had been attracted to someone enough that he wanted to spend his life with her. Now there was this growing need that never left him, to be with Fiona the rest of his life. That need scared him. She had been on his mind from almost the first day he met her. The more he got to know her, the more involved he felt.

He knew she was not doing anything to make him feel trapped. And even though the sex was fantastic, which surprised him at his age, she had not put any holds on him. The only disquieting thing was her wanting to meet Molly.

He knew his daughter would be happy that he had

a girlfriend, and they would like each other. But what if something happened to Fiona? Could he go through that pain again? He knew to love again would be a risk, and he was not sure he wanted to take it. He knew he loved her but was that enough.

At least for now he had some breathing room. Next week he would be with her only a short time. Then that following week they would fly to San Francisco to see Bryan and Diana. Maybe he could come to terms with things after that. He knew that with the timing of their trips he would not have to deal with the issue until after getting back from South America.

Chapter Thirty-Four

True to her words Fiona did not bring up Molly when Devlin came the following weekend. They had such a short time together. He did not get to her condo until after 7:00 p.m. His meeting in Chicago had lasted longer than he had anticipated, but there had been a lot to cover for his upcoming South American trip. At least traffic, once he got out of the city, and the weather had been good on his ride north.

Fiona had made dinner for them because she knew he would not want to go out after his drive. Besides they would be meeting Kathy and Eric the next night for dinner. Since he had promised she could meet Molly after their San Francisco trip, she decided to drop the issue for the present.

"You look tired, Sweetheart."

"Usually I don't mind the drive up here but today I came from downtown so the ride seemed a lot longer."

"How did your meeting go?"

"It went really well. I am going to cruise the bottom half of South America. The cruise line gave my company an excellent deal. I was worried I would have to fly from country to country which gets very tiring. I will miss some of the interior 'hotspots', but at least I will only have to unpack once while I keep moving as you always like to say."

"That is the way I feel when I cruise. Packing and unpacking gets old real fast. I made a tuna fish casserole and salad for dinner. I hope that is okay because I was not sure when you would get here and that is something easy to heat up."

"Anything you fix is wonderful. I appreciate your fixing dinner, and when we are finished I will help you clean up."

As they sat down to dinner Fiona asked, "So where are you flying to…Rio?"

"No, I am flying into Buenos Aires. I get there a couple of days before the cruise which will help me acclimate after the long plane ride. I am going to do a flight-seeing excursion to Iguassu Falls one of the days and a city tour with a stop at Evita's grave the day I board the ship."

"I have always heard how cosmopolitan that city is, and it sure would be fun to go to one of the tango clubs. They are also known for their great restaurants, and since they raise some of the best cattle in the world, don't forget to order a steak. I have never visited there, but it is on my bucket list."

"I have definite plans for a steak dinner. I have already been studying the areas where I am going because we leave for San Francisco Thursday, and there probably will not be a lot of time for research when I return. Also I don't know how well my computer will work in some of those isolated spots."

"That is very true. But changing the subject, I hope we don't wear out our welcome with Diana and Bryan. Ten days seems a long time for a visit."

"You know they insisted we stay that long. And there are so many things to do in that area. They will go to work on some days, so that will give them a break from us."

"The other good thing is we will have a rental car during the week when they are working so we will not be tied down. I am so glad you suggested that, Devlin. Now tell me more about your trip.

"From what I have read the geography on the eastern side of the continent is not too exciting. We make a stop at Montevideo, Uruguay and I cannot find anything of much interest there. Next up will be Patagonia. It is known as a wild region and a backpacker's paradise. By the time we reach that area we will be in penguin territory. I am really looking forward to seeing those creatures."

"I wish I could go with you, but the Mediterranean is calling I was in Ushuaia, which they call 'The End Of The World,' when I did an Antarctic cruise. I don't know if you studied that geography yet, but it is interesting. When you get to the bottom of South America the eastern half is owned by Argentina and the western half by Chile. Before the bottom is an archipelago which is just a group of islands, that are called Tierra del Fuego. The two countries own the area; and Ushuaia, which is the jumping off port for Antarctica, is the capital of the Argentina side."

"I did notice that the Strait of Magellan runs at the bottom of the continent and above Tierra del Fuego."

"Yes and that is the passage most ships take. Everyone thinks ships go around Cape Horn, but that is not practical. The Cape is where the Atlantic and Pacific Oceans meet, and since the winds have few land masses to serve as windbreaks in that part of the world the area can be almost impossible to navigate at times. I know you will hear the phrase 'The Roaring Forties.' Usually between the latitudes of forty and fifty degrees the westerly winds can be very strong. I just hope you have a calm passage and don't experience that."

"After our last cruise I have had enough of strong winds for awhile. Hopefully it will be a smooth sailing."

"You will notice on the Pacific side that the scenery becomes stunning. I did a short cruise after my Antarctic trip up the coast of Chile. There are some beautiful inlets, and I was on a small ship that traversed Glacier Alley. The captain went into several fjords and piloted the ship right up to the land. There were beautiful glaciers on all three sides and that deep blue-green color was awesome. Once you get on the Chile side of South America you start paralleling the Andes, one of the longest mountain chains in the world."

"I did notice Glacier Alley listed on my itinerary. I also read when we get further north we are stopping at a town called Puerto Montt. That is supposedly in the heart of Chile's lake district as well as containing several snow-covered volcanoes and national parks. My editor wants me to take a shore excursion when I get to that area. He thinks it will be interesting enough that I can write a whole article just on that region."

"You are probably right. I know I could write an entire article on Ushuaia."

As he finished eating Devlin continued, "We end the cruise at the port city of Valparaiso. From there it is an eighty mile bus ride up through the mountains to Santiago. Since it is the capital, it is supposedly another very cosmopolitan city. I will fly out of there at midnight, so that should give me a chance to do a city tour and sample some Chilean wines."

"It sounds like a fabulous trip, Devlin. Sometimes it amazes me we are able to travel to these wonderful places while getting paid to do it."

"You are right, Fiona. I certainly got lucky when I found this job."

Smiling at each other they took their dirty dishes to the kitchen and began cleaning up. Fiona asked if he wanted to watch something on TV but he just shook his head “no.”

“I think I would rather go to bed.”

Agreeing with him, Fiona was a little sad. The day was over. She only had one more day before he had to go back to Illinois. At least their trip was coming up at the end of the week, and they would be together for ten days. She was getting so she just hated it when they had to leave each other.

Chapter Thirty-Five

Meanwhile back in Los Angeles, Maxine was living it up. She could not believe she could have as much fun as she was having with Zack taking her to all the hot spots every night.

He had returned on New Year's Eve day as promised, and she had gotten some invitations to some "in" parties. She had become a minor celebrity. After she moved out of the condo into her new quarters, she had met some people who knew Emma. They told everyone living in the place about the tragedy that had befallen her mother.

They knew 'Miriam' had to have money to be living where she was, and so she had been admitted into their higher class circles when her story became known. She let people call her Miriam because she did not want anyone to know about that 'other' person.

She still was a little worried about her money situation. The insurance company was stalling and she was afraid they might wait years to pay off since there was no body. She supposed if she had to she would hire a lawyer to help deal with them. Zack said he might be able to help her with the insurance issue, but she was not sure he could do very much.

She had gotten quite a bit of money from the appraiser she had sold all the contents of the condo to. And Emma's condo had a few nibbles, but there were no offers yet. She needed some serious money from either the insurance or the sale of the condo to support her new lifestyle. It took lots of cash to keep up with the rich and famous.

She slept in every morning since she was out carousing every night. In the afternoons she pampered herself. She had her nails done, a massage or just spent time on retail therapy. Zack would join her every afternoon at 5:00 p.m. for cocktails. As far as she knew he did not know anyone in Los Angeles, but he got upset with her when she questioned what he did all day.

"I spend every night with you, my sweet. Isn't that enough?" She had no idea he was working her case and getting more and more frustrated by the day.

Happy that he wanted to be with her every night was enough for now. And the nightmares had stopped! Since she had moved from the condo Emma no longer called out for her at night. Life was very very sweet.

When Zack suggested they take a little trip, possibly a cruise that included an overnight stay on Catalina Island, she flatly refused him.

"No more cruises, Zack. I could not bear it. And Catalina Island of all places. That is where Natalie Wood drowned." In reality she really would not have minded a cruise except she had an irrational fear that if she sailed on another ship, Emma would get her. She knew that could not happen, but she was so thankful the nightmares had stopped. She did not want anything to trigger them into starting again.

She was not aware that Zack had been taking a lot of heat from the home office. He was one of their top investigators and had saved the company a lot of money on claims over the years. He was becoming very frustrated because he could not get any information out of Miriam.

He knew by the way she acted she was happy Emma was dead, but she never said anything to put her mother down. There was absolutely no proof that she had thrown her overboard. There was a lot of supposition but if she never admitted to anything his company was going to get stuck paying the claim.

They could stall for a while, but eventually they would have to pay out. It was so exasperating to know he was making no progress; besides the lifestyle of a playboy was wearing on him. He hated staying out all night partying and sleeping all morning. A little of that fun went a long way as far as he was concerned.

He could not understand how Miriam could be happy leading such an empty life. But then she had her indulgences in the day time, and his coddling at night. Maybe that was enough for the woman. It certainly was a boring life to him.

Valentine's Day was quickly approaching, and he knew Miriam expected a beautiful night with him. Instead he planned to pick a fight with her. Enough was enough. At this point he could continue to monitor her activities from a distance. He knew if the company paid the claim she would remain an open file on his desk for the rest of his life. Meanwhile he had some other cases that were calling, and he had a feeling they would be a lot more satisfying than following Miriam around all night.

He had been so sure that he could crack her, but nothing he tried had worked. Whenever he brought up Emma's name, she would clamp her mouth shut and refuse to speak about her mother. He finally realized he had to quit asking. It was time to move on to greener pastures.

Chapter Thirty-Six

As Fiona knew it would Saturday had flown by. She and Devlin had gone to a little town near her home that was known for its antique shops. Molly's birthday was coming up, and Devlin wanted to see if he could find something for her house.

Then they had gone to dinner with Kathy and Eric. When they finally returned home they made love, and Devlin quickly fell asleep. Fiona had tears in her eyes thinking about how fast the weekend had passed.

At least there were only five days until their flight to San Francisco. Devlin said good-bye, and she told him she would get to his house about 4:00 p.m. on Wednesday. They were flying out of O'Hare, so she would take the two of them to the airport the following morning and park there. Since they were taking the red eye back, she could jump in her car and get back to Wisconsin on the return. Devlin had already arranged for the shuttle to take him home.

The first three days of the week sped by, and soon she was driving into the parking lot at Devlin's condo. He had planned to pick up some Chinese takeout for dinner since they were leaving about 6:30 a.m. for the airport. Their flight was at 10:00 a.m., but they were not sure how long the security lines at the airport would be. Since she was parking at an off-airport lot, which entailed taking a shuttle to the terminal, they decided more time was better than less.

They spent a quiet evening together. They had both made lists of attractions they wanted to visit while in San Francisco, and decided they would take turns picking places. They were flying business class because the seats were wider, and it was a four hour ride.

Before they knew it the plane was taking off, and they held hands as they soared above the clouds. It had been a very cloudy morning, but as soon as they got above the clouds the sun was shining brightly. They both had brought books, but neither one of them felt like reading. Instead they talked quietly about their upcoming trip.

Since there was a two hour time change, the plane landed in San Francisco at noon. By the time they got to baggage they spied Diana waiting for them.

"Hi, you two. It is so good to see you again," Diana said as she gave both of them a hug.

"We are so glad you invited us," Fiona told her friend as Devlin went to retrieve the luggage. "Where is Bryan?"

"He had to work today. When I am not on an assignment, I have more free time to take off. But he is taking a vacation day tomorrow for our weekend trip to Napa Valley. I am so glad you wanted to do that with us."

"I have been to San Francisco before for some conferences but never had time to do a lot of the touristy things. Devlin has only flown in and out while never visiting the city. Our bosses both agreed to pay our expenses if we come up with at least two articles. From the research I have been doing I don't think that will be too hard."

"Imagine a working vacation," Diana said as the two women laughed.

"Here comes the luggage. I better go help Devlin."

Diana had arranged for a limo service to take them to her home. As soon as they exited the airport baggage the car pulled up.

"Wow, this is a pretty impressive way to travel. I thought we would drag our luggage into the parking lot to your car."

"Actually this limo is on 24 hour hire to our magazine. All I had to do was ask for it far enough in advance. Bryan and I take public transportation a lot. It is easier to get around town that way, and also our condo doesn't have a garage. I haven't owned a car in years. I was out of town so much it did not seem worth the expense. Bryan has a car, but he keeps it at a garage a couple of miles from where we live. We basically use it if we want to go on road trips like Napa this weekend. That is why we told you not to rent a car. You can use ours."

"We did not want to take advantage of you, but since you won't need yours, we can cancel our reservation if you think Bryan won't mind."

"I know he will be happy to let you use it. He has had the car for over ten years. He gets it serviced once a year whether it needs it or not. It only has fourteen thousand miles on it, so you can tell he does not use it much."

As the limo sped towards the downtown, Diana pointed out some of the special sites they were passing. By the time they got to the condo it was almost 2:00 p.m.

Giving the driver a gratuity, she led them up the stairs of their row house. There was a beautiful view of the bay with Alcatraz in the distance. They both guessed that the couple lived in a very prestigious part of town.

"I know you are probably tired but let me show you around the place and then you can put your luggage in your room and come back down and have some snacks. Bryan will not get here until after 6:00 p.m., and you have to be hungry after flying all morning."

The house was typical of the row houses found in the city. Usually there was a garage on the lower level, but instead the previous owners had converted that area into a large office/den because they did not own a car. It made a perfect office for them, and Diana had added a small darkroom to the area.

"After Bryan's divorce he rented, and since he was gone so much, he saved his money and had a good amount in savings by the time we started dating. Early in my career I decided to invest in a condo. It was not in a neighborhood with nice views like this, but it did appreciate over the years. After we got married we pooled our resources and were able to afford this place. We both love it. And since Bryan previously lived in a house with his ex, now he does not have to worry about doing yard work as he did when he owned his own home."

As they entered the hallway there was a staircase to the left. There was a large living room to the right which led into a separate dining room with pocket doors. The house was not very wide, but went back quite a ways. After the dining room there was a kitchen. Beyond that on the left was a small den where they would watch TV together. To the right of the den was a laundry room. Upstairs there were two big bedrooms with a separate bathroom in each of them.

After they put their luggage in their bedroom they joined Diana in the kitchen. She had made some finger sandwiches and a plate with fruit and another one with veggies and dip. She also served iced tea, and they sat eating and talking until Bryan came home.

Bryan had picked up a chicken dinner from a local deli. He did not want Diana to have to worry about fixing dinner when they were going away for the weekend.

He also had his car delivered, and they had luckily found a place to park it on the street right out front. The two couples spent the evening chatting. They were very compatible, and it was if they had known each other for years.

By 9:00 p.m. Fiona could not keep from yawning. It was really 11:00 p.m. Midwestern time, and Bryan suggested they turn in for the night.

They were planning on leaving at 9:00 a.m. the next morning. The trip to Napa only took an hour if you followed the interstate, but Bryan thought they would enjoy following the coast north on Hwy 101 before heading inland.

After a breakfast of blueberry muffins, fruit and cereal they were soon on their way towards the Golden Gate Bridge. Since they were going the opposite way of traffic, they had no trouble crossing the famed structure.

Diana pointed out Sausalito and Muir Woods. They were now on the Redwood Highway, and both Bryan and Diana suggested they come back to this area on one of their free days.

"You will love Sausalito. It is an artist's paradise. You can go over to Muir Woods to see the giant redwoods and then stop in Sausalito for lunch. Even if it is foggy in San Francisco, the sun always shines over here."

They arrived in Napa Valley around lunch time. They stopped at a cute little café, and after lunch checked into the B&B they were staying at for the weekend. The Inn was perfect. It was a huge old home with a wraparound porch, and both of their bedrooms had views of the distant hills as well as hot tubs.

"This place is fantastic Fiona said as she was unpacking. "I hope we have time to enjoy that hot tub."

"I am sure we will. I think Bryan and Diana are thinking the same thing we are."

Within a half hour they were on their way again. Bryan would not say where they were going. It was a surprise! And what a surprise.

Before they knew it the four of them were climbing into a hot air balloon. As they rose into the air the valley with all its wineries stretched out for miles below them.

That was one of the more fun things Fiona ever did, and she knew she would write about the experience. After the ride they went to a restaurant the B&B owner had suggested. They were finished by 8:00 p.m. They all wanted to get back to their rooms and hot tubs.

The next morning they visited the unique shops that lined the street. Then in the afternoon they went wine tasting. The B&B had provided such a big breakfast that they nibbled on cheese and crackers during their tasting sessions and skipped lunch. They did another early dinner and went to their rooms after that. They enjoyed their time together, but at the same time gave each other space. It was the perfect weekend.

Fiona and Devlin were both sad when Sunday arrived and they headed back to San Francisco in the afternoon.

Bryan and Diana were going to take the following Friday off, too. They had told them they would take a trip down to Monterey with an overnight stop in Carmel for that weekend. There was a perfect B&B right on the ocean in Carmel, and Bryan had reserved two rooms for them. They were planning on returning late Saturday evening so they could drop their friends off for their red eye flight home.

Meanwhile they had Monday through Thursday to explore the city. On Monday they signed up for a city tour which included seeing some celebrity homes. They saw Don Johnson's, Danielle Steel's, Robin Williams', and Shirley Temple's homes. The tour gave them a nice overview, and that helped them decide where they wanted to go back to again. Tuesday they took Bryan's advice and went to Muir Woods and Sausalito.

Wednesday and Thursday they spent exploring the city. They went to Fisherman's Wharf and over to Pier 39 to see the harbor seals. Fiona could not believe how loud the barking of the seals was. They rode a streetcar and had lunch in Chinatown. They stopped at a tea garden in Golden Gate Park and after that drove down Lombard Street known as "the crookest street in America."

While they had lunch in Sausalito Fiona mentioned perhaps she should stay over at Devlin's on Sunday, and that way she could meet Molly before she went home. Otherwise it would be weeks before she would again have the opportunity. She almost regretted immediately asking him when she saw the scowl on Devlin's face.

He did not answer her, and she let the subject drop. But during the next two days, even though they were having so much fun sightseeing, she noticed a difference in his demeanor. She thought if she ignored his attitude it would go away, so that is what she did.

Friday night was Valentine's Day, and although they spent a very romantic weekend in Carmel, Devlin still was not acting his usual self. When she finally asked him what was wrong all he said to her was "later."

Before they knew it they were being dropped off at the airport. It had really been a wonderful trip, and they both knew they would miss Bryan and Diana's company. They promised to keep in touch with the couple, and hoped they would be able to see each other again.

When they got to the gate they still had over an hour before their flight. The plane was leaving at midnight and would get into O'Hare at 6:00 a.m. due to the time change. They were flying in the upgrade section with reclining seats, so they would be able to sleep a little. They knew that would be much more comfortable than economy class.

As they sat waiting for their plane Fiona asked, "What is wrong, Devlin? You have not been yourself these last two days."

"Fiona I did not want to talk about this now, but maybe this is the right time with our separate trips coming up."

As she waited for him to keep speaking he continued, "I really enjoy being with you. I even think I love you. Except for the Molly thing you have never put demands on me. But I am afraid to commit. I was in so much pain for so long after Shannon died, and I never want to feel that again. Everyone tells me to take a chance. I know I have felt nothing but joy when I am around you, but I am terrified to take things to the next level."

"Why can't we just continue as we are?"

"It would not be fair to you. I do not think I will ever change my thinking. Since we are going on separate trips and will not see each other for a month anyway this is probably the best time to say good-bye."

"You mean break-up? But I don't understand what you are saying. We just spent ten perfect days together. Why in the world would you want to break-up?"

"I cannot explain why. It is just something I feel."

"Well at least you won't have to worry about introducing me to your daughter."

"That is not fair, Fiona."

"This whole situation is not fair. You throw this at me now when we are both leaving, and you just make the decision all by yourself without even trying to talk it over."

"I am truly sorry. I just feel I need to do this."

Devlin got up and went over to buy a magazine.

When he got back he would not even look at her. She could feel the coldness emanating from him. As far as she was concerned he had totally shut down, and she could feel it.

Neither one of them slept on the way home, but they did not talk to each other either. Fiona had a window seat, and she stared outside at the stars knowing she was in shock. She could not believe it was over. Their relationship had been so wonderful. They had been so compatible and had agreed and laughed at so many of the same things. She knew what Devlin meant about the pain of losing Shannon. She was feeling it now knowing she was losing him.

Happy Valentine's Day she thought to herself.

They walked together from the plane to the baggage area without talking. As soon as she retrieved her bag, without giving Devlin a glance, she walked over to the bus transportation center where the shuttle would pick her up and take her to her car.

She never remembered driving home. It was lucky she did not have an accident. She made it safely inside her condo before she broke down.

Chapter Thirty-Seven

Maxine was not aware she was about to have a lousy Valentine's Day, too. Zack had been acting strangely the last few days, and when she questioned him about why he had just shrugged his shoulders and said "it was nothing."

Actually it was getting harder and harder for him to be around her. He had never liked her, and trying to pretend he did was very trying.

Maxine, of course, had no idea what he was thinking. Even though she paid for everything when Zack was around, she expected he would get her some flowers or candy for Valentine's Day.

As usual they were going to a private party. She would have liked to have had a quiet dinner alone before hitting a nightclub, but Zack had insisted on going to the party.

She was shocked when he arrived to pick her up. He had no flowers nor candy nor even a card. It was almost as if he was deliberately trying to make her angry. But she did not take the bait. Instead she went into her bedroom and got her purse and wrap.

Soon after that the limo dropped them off at the party. When they arrived, there were already well over one hundred people participating in the celebration. It was loud and noisy, and Maxine wished it were quieter so they could chat. But that was not going to happen.

Zack went over to get her a drink, and as she chatted with some friends he disappeared.

Where in the world did he go she wondered? Soon she had her answer. He was dancing very slowly with a woman who could only be described as a "hot babe." She had a slinky, low cut red cocktail dress on, and Zack's hands were all over her backside.

She had no idea the woman was a friend of Zack's and had come to the party as a favor to him. He wanted to break up with Miriam, and he thought this would be a perfect way to do it. He just hoped she would not make a big scene.

When Maxine saw him with the woman she did not know whether to go over and say something, or just wait until it played out. She decided to ignore him for the present since she was talking to some friends.

Everything was fine for about a half hour when one of her "close" friends came over and asked if she had broken up with Zack.

Knowing she could not ignore the situation any longer, she went over to where the couple was dancing.

"Aren't you going to dance with me, Zack? It is Valentine's Day."

"I prefer Cheryl's company to yours, Miriam."

Her mouth dropped. She could not believe what he had just said.

"So you found a new rich younger woman to squire about?"

"That about sums it up. So why don't you run along and play with your 'old' friends."

Maxine was shocked. She could not believe Zack was being so hurtful. Turning back to her friends, she never saw the couple slip out of the party.

What a lousy Valentine's Day she was thinking.

Zack on the other hand was happy to finally be rid of her. He felt such a sense of relief being away from her.

Chapter Thirty-Eight

Fiona was like a zombie all week. She still could not believe Devlin had broken up with her. They had been so compatible and had so much fun with each other. Their time together in San Francisco had been amazing.

She emailed Diana and Bryan thanking them for the wonderful time. She and Devlin had bought them dinner when they were in Carmel, but she knew it was proper to send a thank-you. She did not say anything about splitting up with Devlin. However she did tell Kathy.

Kathy was shocked by the split. She knew Fiona was devastated and was thankful her friend had a job that would take up most of her waking moments. She knew it would take time for the reality to sink in.

Despite the firmness in his attitude, Fiona still spent the week waiting for the phone to ring and for Devlin to say he had been wrong. However that never happened.

Before she knew it she had printed out all her research, gathered up her tour books and finished packing for the overnight plane to Spain. Her company did not fly her first class, but she went business class with the reclining seats that were wider and had more leg room than coach seats.

She wondered if she would be able to sleep on the flight remembering her last journey with Devlin. However, since she had spent sixteen to eighteen hours the last few days getting ready for her assignment, soon after the plane took off she felt herself nodding off.

She awoke just before the aircraft arrived in Germany. She had to change planes, and it was a hassle going through security to get to the correct concourse. She got to the gate with only ten minutes to spare before take-off. However, she had not minded changing planes in Germany.

It felt good to race through the airport after sitting such a long time. She knew the flight was only an hour and a half, and it was a clear day so she could look out the windows to the snow capped Alps below. Before she knew it she arrived in Barcelona.

Knowing she still had a day and a half before her cruise, she was looking forward to touring the city. Fiona took an airport shuttle to her hotel and checked in. After unpacking her overnight bag, changing clothes and taking a quick shower, she was ready for an adventure exploring the city.

Studying the information she had gathered about the town, she knew it would be easy to get around. First she walked to the subway entrance which was just around the corner from her hotel. The subway was a pretty straightforward system that was color coded, and since her hotel was a distance from the downtown area that was where she now headed.

Arriving downtown, she bought a two day ticket for the Hop On & Off Trolley. It was a double-decker bus, and there were headphones which let you pick the language you needed. The first thing she did was ride the bus the entire route to get her bearings. It was even warm enough for her to sit up on the top open area which gave her much better views of the city.

There were several places she wanted to visit the

next day, but for now she jumped off the trolley downtown on the famous La Rambla Street. The area she selected was closed to traffic for a couple of blocks and had been made into a walking mall. There were tapas bars and cafes lining both sides of the street. Musicians, mimes and street vendors were everywhere.

The area was not too busy since it was still afternoon, so she had time to leisurely check out the souvenirs and other mementos for sale before choosing an outdoor café for dinner. As she sat waiting for her meal, she watched the people walk by. Feeling a tiredness descending after the long journey and time zone differences, she went back to her hotel right after eating.

She could not believe it! She slept fourteen hours and had just missed the hotel breakfast. She dressed quickly, stored her luggage with the bellman and was once again heading downtown on the subway. This time she got on and off the trolley to tour Gaudi's famed Church of the Holy Family, the 14th century Gothic Quarter, and the Picasso Museum.

She arrived back at her hotel by 4:00 p.m. The shuttle was leaving for the cruise ship at 4:30 p.m. and would take about fifteen minutes to arrive at the terminal. The ship had a later sailing than normal. It was not leaving until 7:00 p.m., so that had given her plenty of time to explore some of the city sights that day.

Since most passengers had checked in earlier, she found the embarkation process went quickly and smoothly. Upon boarding the ship, she discovered her cabin was a beautiful roomy suite with a balcony off the living room and also off the bedroom. It was so easy to slip into this lifestyle of luxurious cruising even if she did not have a butler this time.

The next day was a day at sea before arriving in Civitavecchia, the port city fifty miles from the Eternal City of Rome. Since she had done a city tour there previously, she decided to try public transportation and took the train to the city. She got off at the stop for Vatican City, and met up with her guide for the walking tour she had purchased in advance. By taking the walking tour she avoided the long lines for tickets that were a given at the Vatican.

She was able to explore several museums, the Sistine Chapel and St. Peter's Basilica on her tour and still had time to catch Rome's Hop On & Off trolley for a quick circuit around this famed metropolis. The only stop she got off for was the Trevi Fountain. You had to walk about a block and a half to get to the fountain, and she wanted to once again toss in a coin to ensure her return to this majestic city.

The trolley dropped her off right at the station, and she was soon speeding back to the ship on the train. She might have worried about not taking the ship sponsored excursion, but since she had been to Rome before she felt confident what she was doing was safe. When she was by herself in Rome she would stand on the fringe of some tourist group, so it did not look as if she was alone.

The cities were once again inland from where the ship docked at the next two ports. Since she was not as familiar with these areas, she took the official ship sponsored tours. The next morning they docked in Piraeus, and she was soon doing a city tour of Athens. There was so much to see. She wished she had more time. The highlight of the tour was the steep walk up the Acropolis to the Parthenon and the Propylea. The buildings were almost surreal in their splendor. Athens was the birthplace of Western civilization, and she could hardly believe she was standing right in the middle of things.

The next stop was Ephesus in southern Turkey. She

had been to Pompeii in Italy before, and the ruins there had been wonderfully excavated and preserved. This archaeological site was a close second and very impressive with the marble paved streets and ruins of the Temple of Hadrian and Library of Celsus.

It seemed amazing to be standing in the amphitheater where St. Paul had preached and to walk through the home where the Virgin Mary had spent her last days. As she exited the house she found herself in a courtyard. While there, she lit a candle in memory of her mother.

After Ephesus there was more time at sea before the overnight stop at Alexandria, Egypt. She had been so busy touring and worn out by the time she returned to the ship each night she had not had much time to think about Devlin. However on the day at sea she spent the daylight hours thinking constantly of him which made her want to cry.

She had no idea he was taking the break up even harder than she was. He thought it would be easier to end things sooner, but it was not long after he had broken things off that he realized this situation was just as painful as losing Shannon. He knew he had been a fool to give up a relationship with someone as wonderful as Fiona. However, he did not know how to fix the situation. Since he was leaving on his three week trek to South America and Fiona was already away, he knew there was nothing he could do for the present.

Fiona was excited when they docked in Alexandria since she had never been to Egypt. The area was a bustling modern city of four million people, but she was not impressed by what she saw. This could be a dangerous area, especially for women alone, so once again she took the ship sponsored excursions.

The first day in port she did the twelve hour tour

to Cairo. This tour included three hours of driving both to and from the city. That left six hours of touring. The drive to Cairo went through the desert, and they left the ship in a convoy of buses with armed motorcycle men surrounding them.

She was riding in the back of the bus as usual when she smelled smoke. All of a sudden the vehicle pulled to the side of the road. Another bus stopped behind them as well as several motorcycle guards. They were told there was something wrong with the motor, and they were to exit the bus and board the other one as quickly as possible. Fiona did not think it took much more than five minutes to do the exchange, and before she knew it they had caught up to the convoy. What efficiency compared to what they had gone through in the Yucatan.

The first stop was the Pyramids of Giza, the Sphinx and a camel ride. Standing in front of those regal monuments took her breath away. Cairo, on the other hand, did nothing for her. They were taken to a nice place for lunch before going to the famous National Museum to see King Tut and other wonders stored there.

The city itself was teeming with people and was very dirty. But when she saw a dead donkey laying in the river and a boy fishing nearby she was glad they had gone to a nice restaurant to eat. She was happy she had a chance to tour Cairo, but this was not a city she cared to ever come back to.

She felt the same way the next day when she did the Alexandria city tour. There were a lot of slums, and it was not the idealized vision she had of this Mediterranean city of Caesar and Cleopatra. Instead the city was dirty and teeming with people. The crew on board had warned them of pickpockets. She usually kept her valuables in a plastic case inside her clothes around her neck. But that morning as she left for the city tour she accidentally put her ship key card in her pocket. Imagine her surprise when she got back to the ship and discovered her card was missing.

She had never felt a thing. Luckily they had not gotten anything of value. She knew whoever had taken it would be upset when they thought they had stolen a credit card and instead only had a keycard that opened a cabin door on board some cruise ship. However this incident added to her dislike of the city.

The cruise was coming to an end. There was only one more port of call, the small island of Malta. This island had played an important role during the Crusades and was full of medieval castles, palaces and beautiful churches.

Instead of doing a city tour, which included an excursion to the city of Mdina, she had asked a couple on board whom she had dined with if they would like to split the cost of a taxi that included a city tour. This was much cheaper than the ship excursion, and even though she was not paying for the tour out of her own pocket, she thought it would be more interesting to explore the sites with a local guide without all the crowds from the ship.

Finally they were on the last day at sea before their return to Barcelona. Fiona spent much of the time at her sitting room desk organizing all the notes she had made. She knew she had enough information to write several articles. At least that would keep her busy when she returned home.

She knew Devlin would be off to South America. Even though she still ached for him, the reality of their break up was becoming easier for her to accept. She knew she would never again find someone she would let down her guard with, and she was now resigned to spending her life alone.

Chapter Thirty-Nine

Home again. It was now mid March, and the weather was still cold but at least the days were lengthening. Fiona worked on her articles and went out with friends, but she did not go to dinner with Kathy and Eric on Saturday nights any more. That would remind her too much of Devlin.

Her editor had sent her on a couple of short assignments, and before she knew it summer was approaching. Once again she decided to only submit articles, and not travel as she had done the previous year. She wanted to spend the summer boating on Lake Michigan with her friends.

And she had met a man. Well, sort of. Jerry was a friend of Eric's and had been a year ahead of them in school. Fiona had not known him when they were kids. He had recently lost his wife and was having a hard time getting over his loss.

When you are alone it often feels like you are single living in a couple's world, and Eric had felt it might ease his friend's pain a little to have someone as a friend to do things with. She found herself coupled with Jerry more and more over the summer. However, Fiona insisted that she pay her own way. She did not want to lead him on or let him think she might be romantically inclined towards him.

Frankly, he had started getting on her nerves somewhat. He constantly talked about his wife and the things they used to do, and she worried he was not dealing with her death well. The situation reminded her a little of the way her mother had been after losing Fiona's dad.

The worst incident was on the 4th of July. For some reason Fiona kept thinking of Devlin that day. She knew they would have had such a fun summer together. She did not know why her thoughts were on him since she worked at not thinking about their time together.

She remembered her mother always saying when you think about someone out of the blue they are probably thinking of you at the same time. She wondered if Molly had her baby yet. Maybe that was why she was thinking of Devlin.

Meanwhile Jerry was slowly ruining her day. He spent the whole afternoon reliving every 4th of July he had spent with his wife. Fiona did not want to be rude, but she finally began to tune him out. By the time the boat docked it was 6:00 p.m., and pleading a migraine, she went home. Knowing she would start screaming if she had to listen to one more story, she had to get away from him.

Heating up some soup, she poured a glass of wine and sat on her couch watching the waves roll in. When darkness descended and the fireworks began she sat out on her balcony and watched the spectacle. Not having people talking around her was very peaceful after listening to Jerry all day. She continued going out with him for Eric's sake, but only on weekends when her friends were also around. She wanted to slowly distance herself from him because she knew the relationship was going nowhere.

She continued to email Diana so she could keep up with their news. She had finally told her friend about Devlin leaving her. Diana was as shocked as everyone else by the news. The couple was taking a vacation and had decided to come visit her for a few days in August. They had never been to Wisconsin and loved being with her. When they left they told her they wished they could have stayed longer.

Diana also told her a new story in the Miriam saga. Bryan had to go to Los Angeles for a convention. He was out one night with friends at a nightclub, and he spotted Miriam.

"You won't believe what happened, Fiona. Bryan went over to say hello. He said she looked a lot different from the old Miriam with her hair and makeup updated. And she was wearing very sophisticated clothes. She also had a 'boy-toy' hovering nearby."

Fiona laughed at the thought of Miriam carrying on with some young stud.

"When Bryan asked if they had ever found her mother she snapped at him and wanted to know why he needed that information. He apologized and said he and I were very sad about her loss, and since he had run into her, he just wanted to know if she was doing all right. She then told him she was doing fine and abruptly turned away from him."

"Wow. That really was a strange encounter."

Diana then asked her if she wanted to talk about Devlin, but she said "no." It was over and done with, and she never wanted to think about him again. Diana decided not to tell her they were going to visit him after they left Wisconsin. There seemed no point in mentioning the fact.

After they left Fiona they drove down to Evanston. When they arrived at his condo, they were shocked by how sad Devlin looked.

"Do you want to talk about it?" Bryan asked after Diana had left for the guest bedroom to unpack.

"Not really, there isn't a lot to say. I made a huge mistake letting her go. My friend, Roy, and my daughter were really upset when I told them about her. I would not have said anything, but they kept asking me what was wrong. They thought perhaps I was sick with some disease since I lost some weight."

"Why don't you call her?"

"She has probably gotten on with her life and does not need me interfering again."

"She has not gotten on with her life. She told Diana she has some friend she goes out with when she needs a partner but she is not interested in ever having another serious relationship. Personally I think she is just as unhappy as you look."

"Let's just drop the subject. It's over."

And with that, there was no more mention of Fiona. The couple had fun with Devlin going to the city and visiting some of the museums. All too soon it was time for them to return home. Saying good-bye when he dropped them at the airport, they promised to keep in touch.

They were so happy with their marriage. They wished everyone could be as content as they were. The fact that Devlin was making the biggest mistake of his life by refusing to reestablish ties with Fiona made them very sad.

"How foolish," Diana said to her husband as their plane lifted into the air.

Chapter Forty

It had been over eight months since Fiona and Devlin had split. She had a feeling she would never want to celebrate Valentine's Day again. It still hurt when she thought about the break-up which she tried to do as little as possible. Returning to Europe in September, she spent six weeks there. It had been a good choice because nothing in those areas reminded her of Devlin.

After being back a few days, she heard some distressing news. Jordan, her managing editor, had called about a so-called reunion in Los Angeles of the travel writers. The cruise ship company had been very impressed with the feedback from all of the writers' articles. They were unveiling a new ship to the Mexican Riviera and wanted all the writers to sail with them on the ship's maiden voyage.

It would be fun to see everyone again. Everyone, that is, except Devlin. She and Diana still kept in frequent contact, and she was curious if Miriam would be joining them.

Diana had spent many lonely years building her career, and now she was so happy with Bryan. She still felt distressed that Devlin had broken up with Fiona the way he had. She was thinking about the new cruise when her phone rang. She was looking forward to seeing Peter and Brody again but wondered if the situation might prove somewhat embarrassing around Fiona and Devlin.

Picking up the phone, she heard her friend say, "I hope you are going on the cruise with everyone."

"Yes, I am. Bryan got permission to take me along. But what about you?"

"I thought about saying 'no' but then decided that would be ridiculous. I refuse to spend so much negative energy being upset by Devlin. It may be a little uncomfortable when we meet again, but hopefully we will get past that awkwardness quickly. Do you know for sure if he is coming on the trip?"

"Bryan called him yesterday, and he verified he was coming."

"Well that is that then. I know Peter and Brody will come but what about Miriam?"

"I know something more about her. Bryan is friends with some people at Miriam's old magazine. I guess she quit writing articles after she got back from Florida."

"I wondered when I had not read anything by her recently."

"The friend said Miriam has been living it up since Emma's death. She still has not sold her mother's condo. There were some maintenance issues she had to take care of first, but supposedly she now has an accepted offer. However, it will be another six weeks before she closes. The insurance company has vacillated paying her off since there is no body. I guess she hired an attorney to force a settlement."

"How in the world did Bryan ever find out all that information?"

"Even though Miriam had given her notice and quit work someone at the magazine did not know, and had sent her the email about all of us getting together again. She called her old editor. She is close to getting some serious money. Since her cash reserves are low right now she told him she would do the cruise. She won't be spending much while on the ship. And since it sails out of Los Angeles, she will not have to fly anywhere."

"That is amazing. I wonder if she will be nice to us or as rude as she was to Bryan. Do you think she will bring along her young stud?"

"I guess we will just have to wait until we board the ship to get those answers."

"I am really looking forward to seeing you and Bryan again. Devlin is another story. If I pretend we are just friends as we were previously hopefully everything will work out all right. After all you two are the only ones who know we had a romantic relationship."

"I had forgotten that. The circumstances may not be as uncomfortable as I had thought since the others do not know anything happened between you two. See you soon, Fiona."

Fiona put down the phone and started to think about the situation of meeting Devlin again. She realized they both would be uncomfortable when they first met. She was hoping it would not happen until the lifeboat drill when she would be surrounded by lots of people.

After all if you try to find a way to live life problem free, you will have to wait a long time, if not forever. Then while you are waiting life will pass you by. So, too, would all the endless, exciting possibilities. It is important to seize opportunities as they occur because that is when magic can and will happen.

Devlin was definitely a problem. If she could get past the awkwardness of their first encounter, the rest of the cruise should be a lot of fun. She was not sure how Miriam would act, but she had a feeling the camaraderie they all shared with Peter and Brody would still be there.

Chapter Forty-One

Time to cruise. Fiona's plane touched down in Los Angeles at noon. Bryan and Diana were arriving about the same time. Since they were flying the same airline, they agreed to meet down at baggage. It was not long before she spied the couple, and much to her surprise Brody and Peter showed up a few minutes later.

They all started talking excitedly back and forth, and it was as if they had just been together yesterday. The old closeness was still there. The five of them decided to go to the ship in the same vehicle. Brody had ordered a limo to take Peter and him to the ship, and he invited the others to ride along.

They chatted all the way to the cruise terminal. When the limo pulled up it was obvious that the cruise line had been waiting for the two men. A woman came running out, and swooping all five of them up transferred them to the first class lounge while she got everyone checked in.

A porter had come for their luggage, and within ten minutes they were all headed for their suites. Fiona could not believe it! When she got to her cabin her bags were already there. She knew the average cruiser would not have the same efficiency when it came to their bags.

Her room was very similar to the suite she had on her Mediterranean cruise. As she started to unpack she realized she had forgotten all about Devlin. That was a good thing. It was almost 2:00 p.m., and that is when they had agreed to meet in the hallway to go to the buffet for some food.

No one wanted a lot to eat, but they agreed they needed something to tide them over for dinner. This ship, like their other one, had anytime dining. Brody had asked the cruise line if they could have a table reserved throughout the cruise at 7:30 p.m. as they had on their previous cruise.

After getting their food they went outside to the area similar to where she and Devlin had gone on the first cruise. It was quieter out there, so they could better chat with each other. There was no sign of Miriam or Devlin, but they had been told the other two would definitely be joining them on the cruise.

As they were talking about their last cruise together they all turned towards Fiona when they heard her gasp. They followed the direction she was looking and saw a slim woman dressed all in black and beautifully made-up.

Fiona realized as soon as she saw her that it was Miriam. She probably would have never guessed if Diana had not told her previously Miriam had changed.

"Standing up, she looked at the woman in greeting and giving her a hug said, "Wow, Miriam, you look fantastic."

"Does that mean I looked bad before?"

"I am sorry. I did not mean to imply that. It is just that you look so sophisticated."

Meanwhile Brody and Peter were looking at the woman with their mouths wide open.

"Since my mother died, I have reinvented myself, so to speak. I don't know if you will be able to remember, but I like to be called Maxine now."

Everyone nodded at her words, but Fiona knew she

would forget.

"I am off to unpack; but I thought you might all be here, so I wanted to come by and say hello. I will see you all at the lifeboat drill. Isn't Devlin coming on this cruise?"

Brody, taking command as usual, answered the woman. "He is scheduled to be here. I am not sure where he is. Maybe his plane is late."

And that was exactly Devlin's problem.

No one saw him at the lifeboat drill, and Fiona wondered if he had cancelled. Perhaps that would be for the best. She was so comfortable around everyone else. Not being uptight if Devlin were there, would be a plus.

They were supposed to sail at 5:00 p.m. However, they heard an announcement from the cruise director that the ship would be a few minutes late departing due to several people boarding from a late plane. As they were enjoying the sailaway party Miriam joined them. She told everyone she had just seen about twenty people board the ship just before it left the dock.

Miriam, no I mean Maxine, Fiona thought to herself was in a very good mood. She was drinking but in moderation. Although everyone knew he was gay, Peter seemed quite taken with her. It was fun to watch him flirt with her. And she was flirting right back.

Diana whispered to Fiona, "We have barely left the dock and already this trip is getting interesting."

Smiling at her friend, Fiona nodded in agreement.

At 7:00 p.m. everyone went back to their cabins to freshen up for dinner. It was not long before they were all entering the dining room.

As they got close to their table Fiona could feel herself tense up. There was Devlin. She was so hoping he had cancelled, but obviously that was not the case. She nodded at him and sat down a couple of seats away from him. Not only was she not next to him, but she was also not across from him. When she looked up, she could not see him without turning her head. Miriam and Peter had taken seats right next to each other which made Fiona smile.

Everyone else was so busy greeting Devlin, that no one except Diana noticed anything different about her friend. She knew it would be a long night for Fiona.

Since she was not sitting close to him, dinner was not as uncomfortable as Fiona thought it might have been. After the meal they all decided to go for a nightcap in the piano bar. It had been a long day with time changes for most of them, and they wanted to turn in early. Brody had slipped into the role of "chairman" once again. He suggested they meet for a working breakfast by the pool at 8:30 a.m.

As she got up to leave the table she heard Devlin say, "May I speak to you for a moment, Fiona?"

As she turned towards him she realized everyone else had already left. There was nothing she could do except look at him. However, before he said anything, she interrupted him.

"Look, Devlin, Bryan and Diana are the only ones who even knew we had an affair. No one else is aware of the fact. So as long as we just act like friends, as we did on the Bahamas cruise, no one will ever know there was anything between us. However, I would rather not pair up with you on shore excursions. Maybe we can somehow get around that."

Watching Fiona standing there with so much hurt in her eyes, made him want to leave the ship immediately. Realizing he could not do that he just nodded in agreement as she turned and walked away.

Seeing her again had made his heart leap. He had been such a fool. It felt so natural to be around her once more. It was as if the months of separation had never happened. Being near each other again brought back all the things he missed about her...her lips, her smile, her laughter.

He could not believe he had forced her out of his life. And yet he had. Roy and Molly were right. He had been idiotic and had mishandled everything. In hindsight, he realized he should have called Fiona when Bryan had suggested it in August.

Why did he ever let things get so out of hand? He could not blame her for not wanting to be around him. If there was any way he could win her back, he would never leave her side. He knew he needed to give her the space she asked for, but somehow he had to spend time with her. If he did not at least try to win her back, he would never succeed.

We have a limited time on earth. He finally realized what he had recently read was exactly how he felt. You need to forgive quickly, kiss and make-up, laugh together and love deeply. And finally, never regret being with someone who makes your heart smile. I cannot change what is past but it is important to move forward.

He did not want to waste anymore time. He would do anything he could to get Fiona back into his life. He was not sure how he would accomplish that, but maybe Bryan could help him.

In order to have a bright future with her they both needed to forget the past failures and heartache. He knew, however, she would not trust him as easily this time. Winning her back was not going to be simple. But he was determined to try.

Chapter Forty-Two

It was 5:00 a.m., and Maxine was exhausted. Her happy life was changing. Events seemed to be spiraling out of control the last few weeks. She did not know how to adjust to this new state of affairs.

First she had caught Jorge rifling through her jewelry. She immediately kicked him out of her house and her life. Then about three weeks previously a very disturbing event had taken place. She had just left a late lunch with some friends when she ran into Zack.

"If you think just because I am in-between men that I will take you back," she said scornfully to the man, "you have another thing coming."

She was shocked when he looked at her with utter contempt. "Listen, doll, I was never interested in you. I am an insurance investigator, and I know you killed your mother. I am the reason your settlement has been hung up. I know you hired a lawyer, and eventually we will have to pay out on the claim. But let me tell you, I plan to haunt you for the rest of your life. If I stay on you as I plan, maybe my company will get a chance eventually to reclaim some of the money even if we have to pay you first."

Her jaw dropped at his words. She turned around quickly and walked away from him. Just what I need she thought—someone else haunting me. When she reflected on all the money she spent on him, she was livid. She hated being used. Emma had emotionally abused Miriam for years, and she had no intention of letting anyone do that to her.

When she saw the email for the writing assignment she had jumped at it. She could always use a little extra cash for incidentals until the condo sold in six weeks. Not only would she control her spending on shipboard, but more importantly she would be away from Zack.

A week later she met a new "boy toy." Before starting this current relationship, she had him thoroughly checked out. Her friend who did the background checks confirmed Raul was okay. She knew she would be leery anytime a new man entered her life from now on after what Zack had said and done to her.

She was sorry she had not brought Raul along on the cruise, as he was very entertaining. At first she had thought it would be better if he did not come along. But the previous night when they all went to the piano bar, she saw Zack! With a smirk he raised his glass in a toast to her.

She could not believe he was on the ship. She was furious and excused herself from the group pleading a headache. Before that incident she had been having so much fun flirting with Peter. She went to bed as soon as she got back to her suite, but in the middle of the night the nightmares with Emma wearing her pink prom dress came back to haunt her. She wondered if Raul had been there would she have avoided the horrifying dreams while sleeping in his arms.

Now it was 5:00 a.m., and she had a pounding headache. She still heard Emma's voice in her head telling her how much she missed her. At one point she remembered yelling out, "For heaven's sake you died in the Atlantic Ocean. Leave me alone. You are in the wrong ocean, Emma."

As her head continued to pound she hoped she was not losing it just when she was coming into a large fortune.

Chapter Forty-Three

Fiona was having a hard time remembering to call Miriam by her new name, but she noticed no one else even tried. It had been a rather strange request to begin with.

At breakfast Brody began handing out shore excursion assignments like he had on the last cruise. Naturally she was being paired with Devlin.

"Listen, Brody, do you really think this is necessary? Most of these shore excursions are city tours, snorkeling or diving, and seeing local sites. We have done all of these tours time and again in the past. Why don't we just pick whatever interests us, and then we can meet and let each other know what we thought. Especially if there is something of interest to critique. As for the ship activities how different can the art auction or wet T-shirt contest be from previous sailings?"

"I agree with Fiona," Bryan concurred. "Tonight is the captain's cocktail party. Between that and dinner we can discuss any relevant issues that come up today. As far as the art auction, after Devlin's experience, I don't care if I ever go to another one."

Peter and Brody looked at each other and nodded their heads in agreement. Miriam was not happy with the situation because she did not want to be alone. She worried Emma or Zack might try to stalk her. She decided she would stick with Peter if he would have her. Being around someone should help keep her mind off of her problems.

Devlin was also not happy with the new state of affairs. How could he win Fiona back if he never got a chance to be with her except when everyone else was around? However, knowing he was out voted, he quickly agreed. He knew Diana was having a massage later in the morning, and he had asked Bryan to join him for coffee.

When the two men met, Bryan was not sure what to say.

"Until I found Diana I was not the greatest with relationships. I know if you try and talk to her after what you just told me she said at the table last night, you will probably strike out. You need to get her alone where she cannot just walk away. Let me talk to Diana. Maybe she will have some ideas. But I want you to know, we will both do anything we can to help you two get back together."

Thanking his friend, Devlin decided maybe he just needed to let fate take over. After all he firmly believed it was fate that had brought them together on that second cruise. Feeling better than he had in a long time he went off to listen to the port talks.

The ship was on a seven day Mexican Riviera cruise. It would cruise down to the farthest port of Acapulco before heading north again. When they arrived in Acapulco Diana, Bryan and Devlin all took the city tour. Fiona had done the tour previously which included a stop at LaPerla to see the famous cliff divers.

Deciding to skip the city tour, she chose instead to just walk around the old town and visit some of the churches and older buildings. Although there could be problems in Mexico, the downtown area was heavily guarded with armed police. The city wanted to do everything in their power to keep the tourists protected. As long as she took normal precautions, such as not wearing fancy jewelry or flashing money, she knew she would be safe.

Peter and Brody had arranged for a specialized tour. They were going to several famous restaurants and check out the food and drinks. Miriam had asked if she could tag along, and they had agreed. She wondered if Zack would follow them, and it was not too soon after they left that she saw the detective. All throughout the day, she kept running into him. The only saving grace was that Peter and Brody had no idea what was going on.

After they returned to the ship Devlin was hoping Fiona would show up for a glass of wine before dinner. But that did not happen. She would have liked to spend time with Bryan and Diana, but they liked to dance and that might leave her alone with Devlin if he turned up. Since she did not want to talk to him, to be safe, she decided not to go.

So he did not see her until dinner time. He was hoping to sit next to her. But everyone took the same seats as the first night, and he did not want to push things. The conversation was lively, and after dinner they went as a group to the theater which was featuring music from Broadway shows. They had settled into a nightly routine, so the piano bar was next. A man dressed like Elvis entered the bar right after they did, and soon everyone was singing Elvis songs.

Fiona noticed that Miriam/Maxine had seemed very distracted during dinner. By the time she arrived at the piano bar she seemed fearful about something and kept looking over her shoulder. When Fiona said something to her, she shrugged her shoulders and said it was nothing. But she was definitely jumpy and was not her usual bubbly self. Even though she was wearing make-up, she looked pale.

Maybe she would feel better in the morning. Tomorrow they were docking at Ixtapa-Zihuatanejo.

Zihua, as it was called, was mostly undiscovered until the Mexican government decided to create a tourist paradise out of a nearby spit of land known as Ixtapa. Fiona decided since she was not interested in water sports that she would take the shore excursion to Troncones.

Researching the area she had learned Troncones was 16 miles north of Zihua. The rugged coastline was known as one of the best surfing spots in all of Mexico. It was also the site for sea turtle nests, virgin beaches and tide pools. Above the beaches a short hike up the mountainside took you to La Majahua caverns and the zip line platforms where you could soar above the jungle on rope harnesses.

And that was exactly what she wanted to try. She was not sure what Devlin would pick as a shore excursion, but she knew the others would not be interested in zip lining. She had never done it before and thought it might be fun to try.

The next morning she boarded the bus and went to a seat in the back. She watched as all the couples filed in filling up all the other seats. It looked as though she would have a seat to herself. Oh, no! She looked up as the guide entered the bus and saw a man right behind him. It was Devlin! How could she be so unlucky? Not only would he be on the tour with her, but the only seat available was right next to her.

He never saw Fiona until he got close to the back of the bus. He smiled to himself. Maybe fate was going to intervene again.

Asking him not to talk to her, she immediately picked up her book. When they got to the mountain she walked ahead of him. He was not sure how he was going to speak to her, but he knew this was the chance he had been waiting for. No matter what happened, he was going to make her listen.

Once again fate took a hand. They had finished zip lining, which she had loved, and she was presently sitting on a concrete bench overlooking the sea when she heard a scream. Turning around she saw a woman falling. When she landed, even from a distance, Fiona could tell her leg did not look right. They were supposed to be returning to the ship in fifteen minutes, but the guide told everyone they would be there a little longer until help arrived.

As she turned to look back at the ocean Devlin knew this was his opportunity. He hurried over and sat beside her on the bench.

She started to rise quickly, but he reached for her arm with his hand.

"Please sit down, Fiona. I need to talk to you. I know you don't want to speak to me after what I did to you. But I want you to know breaking up with you was the biggest mistake I ever made in my life. There is not a single day I don't think about you and miss you."

Rolling her eyes at what he said, he took her hands in his and continued. "I know you don't trust what I am telling you. Why should you after what I did to you. I wanted to call you so often."

"Why didn't you call?"

"I was so wrong. By the time I realized I wanted to be with you, I had convinced myself you had gone on to another life and were probably happier without me."

"But even if we got back together, what would keep you from doing the same thing again in the future. I loved you. Perhaps I should not have pushed about seeing Molly, but your refusal to introduce me was an indication you were not serious about our relationship."

"You are right about Molly. I was afraid of commitment, and so I kept you away from her. I thought that way if we broke-up, she would never know about you. What can I do to make it up to you? I love you, Fiona. I would marry you tomorrow if you would have me."

Fiona gasped. "Marry me? You cannot possibly mean that, Devlin."

"I am totally serious. Please marry me, Fiona."

As he spoke his eyes never left her drawing them closer together. A breathtaking moment passed between them astonishing in its sexual implications. The connection they were experiencing was so intense, it could not be denied. She quickly stood up, and he followed.

Turning her towards him, they both felt an overwhelming desire to touch each other. He could not stand it anymore. He gathered her up in his arms, and held her so tight it hurt. He buried his face in her hair and smelled the scent of her perfume. He then leaned back and as he looked at her, he moved closer until their lips met. Without thinking what she was doing, she encircled her arms around his neck. At the same time his hands reached around her waist, and he pulled her even tighter. It felt so right to be holding her again.

She did not mind the tightness of his hug. She needed the contact and the warmth of his embrace. As he was holding her, she wrapped her arms even tighter around his neck.

"Fiona, I have not been able to get you out of my mind since I left you. You are even in my dreams," he murmured as the kiss ended. "We were meant to be together. Give me another chance. I won't disappoint you.

Looking at him she said, "I never imagined I could find passion like this at my age. I did not consider there could be someone like you out there for me. I don't want you to ever stop kissing me. When you touch me, you make me feel so alive."

As they continued talking they heard the guide ask everyone to board the bus.

Fiona could not believe they had found their way back to each other. They held hands all the way back to the ship while Devlin thanked the powers to be that she had returned to him.

As they were boarding the ship, still holding hands, they ran into Bryan and Diana. The other couple was ecstatic they were back together.

Agreeing to meet for drinks, they went to their cabins to clean up.

Chapter Forty-Four

The boat departed the port at 4:00 p.m. They had a distance to travel until their next destination of Cabo San Lucas. After freshening up the two couples met for their pre dinner wine. Not wanting to talk about Devlin and her reuniting, after the waiter brought their drinks, Fiona asked, "Has anyone researched the next port?"

Bryan answered. "Since we don't dock until 10:00 a.m., I thought I would look over my notes in the morning. Diana and I are doing some water sports for which the area is known."

Fiona resumed, "Well let me tell you a few things I read. Cabo is a party town and has a population of around 70,000 which is small for a Mexican city. You always read about Jennifer Aniston, Cindy Crawford and George Clooney spending time in the area. In the winter months it is fun to take a boat out to see the whales that migrate there. John Wayne and Bing Crosby visited for the sport fishing which is supposed to be the best in the world."

"Don't forget El Arco," Devlin chimed in. "It is one of the last two rocks that mark 'land's end,' at the tip of the Baja peninsula. Basically, El Arco is a big rock with a wide arch cut through it by years of tides and sea. Together the two rocks look like little sharp mountains emerging from the sea and thousands of pictures have been taken or painted of them."

Fiona nodding in agreement continued, "We must not forget the rock 'n' roll roots of the town either. I would like to go visit Sammy Hagar from Van Halen's rock group at his Cabo Wabo Cantina. I don't think I want any tequila, but I might want to buy a shirt in the gift shop. October is the month Sammy is in residence, and we might get a chance to meet the rocker in person. That would be fun."

"Well, I guess that decides it," Devlin said with a twinkle in his eyes. "We will probably just roam around town tomorrow. We are not in port very long, and we have to tender, so I don't think there will be much time for a lot of other things."

Soon it was time for dinner, and the two couples went to the table together. The other three writers were already there and laughing it up.

"We have been to the martini tasting," Peter said with a grin.

"I can tell," Devlin responded as he maneuvered around the chairs so he could sit next to Fiona.

Even though she was laughing, Fiona noticed that Miriam did not look well. Darn, I will never get used to calling her Maxine even though she seems so different from the old Miriam.

Since she was sitting next to her, Fiona leaned over and asked her how she felt.

"I am fine. I just have had trouble sleeping. I keep remembering what happened to Emma on the last cruise. I probably should not have come. I have been 'spooked' on cruising since it happened. I thought if I came I would overcome my apprehension."

"Is there anything I can do to help?"

"No thanks, Fiona. There are just three more nights at sea, and then we will be home. But I realize now I will probably never take another cruise."

"Well, that is certainly understandable."

Soon the food was served, and all conversation died down as they concentrated on eating. Tonight was steak and lobster night and Peter had ordered both entrees.

After dinner they went to the show which featured dancing. As long as it was not comics or magicians Fiona was happy. Later at the piano bar, whenever a slow song was playing, Devlin asked her to dance. Brody thought it was a little strange. He had the feeling the two of them had been avoiding each other, but maybe it was just his imagination since the way they were dancing together tonight seemed very intimate.

Miriam, pleading a headache, left soon after they arrived without even ordering a nightcap.

"There is something weird going on with her," Peter commented. "All day today she barely ate anything at the restaurants we went to, and she kept looking over her shoulder as if someone were following her."

"It is probably because she is thinking about her mother. She told me today she almost did not come because of her mother's tragic death. She thinks she will never go on another cruise."

"From what I have heard when she finally gets all her money she can probably charter her own jet when she wants to travel."

"Do I detect a little jealousy," Brody asked Peter.

"Enough about Miriam. Let's dance Fiona," Devlin murmured as he whispered in her ear.

No one noticed, but when Maxine left the bar Zack got up and followed her. He never said anything but smirked at her when she turned and said, "Quit following me." Realizing nothing would change she turned and went to her cabin as quickly as possible. Imagine her surprise when she looked down the hall and saw him go into the suite right next to hers.

Somehow I have to get through these next couple of nights she was thinking. But as she opened her door she could have sworn she saw a woman in a pink dress heading for the balcony.

Chapter Forty-Five

No one saw Miriam at breakfast the next day. Although they had not made specific plans, they had all congregated by the pool each morning. Peter mentioned Miriam had not asked if she could join Brody and him on their excursion into town. "I wonder if she is going to leave the ship today She did not look very well last night."

Soon they were docked, and the tendering process had begun. Miriam was soon forgotten. It was kind of a lazy day for Fiona and Devlin. They made it to Cabo Wabo. Although he was there they were told Sammy was sleeping, so they did not get a chance to meet him. After the cantina Devlin was resolute about stopping at a jewelry store.

He insisted on buying her a ring if she found the right one. "But then everyone will find out we are engaged," she said.

"I want the world to know," he replied with a big grin. After the night we spent together last night, marriage to you cannot happen soon enough. Although they retained their own staterooms, Devlin wanted to sleep with her each night and had packed a small bag and moved over to her room.

They were looking over the diamonds when a beautiful sapphire ring caught her eye. When she tried it on, it fit perfectly. It would not need to be sized. Devlin bought the ring and slipped it on the fourth finger of her left hand as soon as the purchase was complete.

"Now we are properly engaged."

Fiona kept looking down at the ring. She could not believe how beautiful it was. She had loved the setting as soon as she had seen it. I wish I could tell my mother about Devlin she thought in a moment of sadness. Kathy will certainly be surprised.

When they arrived for their before dinner drink, Diana spotted the ring immediately. "I guess this means you are officially engaged," she said smiling at the blissful couple.

Going into dinner, Peter also spotted the ring right away.

"Wow, you sure work fast, Devlin. Congratulations."

Brody also congratulated them.

"When is the wedding?"

"Everything has happened so quickly we have not had time to make plans," Fiona said blushing. "Where is Miriam?"

"She isn't here yet. I don't think she left her cabin today," Peter said.

"Do you think she is all right?"

"Sure, what could be wrong with her?"

"She has been acting very strange lately, and she looked so peculiar last night. She never even stayed for a nightcap. I know she has been thinking about her mother's death ever since she boarded the ship."

"Don't worry. She is fine. Now let's order dinner," Peter grumbled.

Miriam never came to dinner. It put a pall on their table when they realized she was not going to join them.

After dinner they headed for the show. Tonight there was a magician which Fiona knew she would not enjoy.

“”Devlin, I am going to skip the show. I want to check on Miriam. I am worried about her.”

“I’ll come with you. I have never cared much for magicians either.”

It was not long before the two of them were rapping on her door. There was no response. As they continued knocking a man came out of the room next to Miriam’s.

“Is there a problem?”

Fiona answered, “Our friend did not come to dinner, and we have not seen her all day. We are worried about her.”

Knowing he had not seen her either Zack said, “Perhaps we should find someone to open the door to make sure she is safe.”

“Can we do that? I know I would sleep better tonight knowing she is all right. She had some serious problems on her last cruise and I know she was having a hard time handling some issues on this one.”

“I can go get the room attendant. I saw him just down the hall a few minutes ago.”

Since he was still preparing one of the suites for the evening, he came quickly down the corridor to Miriam’s door. When Fiona explained the situation to him, he said, “She did not let me in to clean this morning. She has had her ‘Do not disturb’ button on all day.”

The three of them stood back in the hallway while the room attendant opened the door. It was dark and the room was very cold since the balcony door was wide open.

Turning on the lights, they went into the bedroom. Miriam was lying in the bed, and she appeared to be in a semi comatose state. She was moaning, and Fiona heard her say 'Emma', 'pink', 'Zack' and 'Miriam', her own name. She was white as a ghost. They called the ship's doctor who felt she was probably dehydrated. He had no idea she had not slept in days because of the nightmares about Emma.

The doctor had a portable I-V sent to the suite which he hooked up to her. He also gave her a sedative intravenously. There was a dancer who had broken her arm and they recruited her to sit with Miriam overnight.

Fiona was filled with relief knowing Miriam would be watched over during the night.

Once everything was under control the man named Zack left. Thanking the room attendant for his help, Devlin followed Fiona to her suite. They both decided they would skip the piano bar that evening. With all that had happened that day they both wanted some quiet time together.

As she lay in Devlin's arms Fiona wondered if Miriam would be better in the morning.

Chapter Forty-Six

As they left for breakfast they stopped to see how Miriam was doing. Between the fluids and sedative the dancer reported that Miriam had settled down into a troubled sleep about an hour after the I-V fluids were administered. The doctor had already been by and had said he thought even though she was having a restless sleep she was no longer in that comatose state. He continued to keep her hooked up to the I-V and had also administered another sedative.

"The doctor said she would sleep until early afternoon. He is sending someone else to relieve me so I can get some sleep. Since this is our last night at sea, I will come back this evening to watch over her. Why don't you plan to come visit her after lunch today?"

"We will definitely do that. I just wanted to make sure she was okay."

When they got to the pool area, the others were already there having breakfast. Fiona filled them in on Miriam's condition. They were all shocked, and told her how glad they were she had gone to check on her.

They had a leisurely breakfast but then left to go their separate ways. There were a lot of activities that day since this was a day at sea. Devlin wanted to go to the shops since they always had sales going on the last day on board. He wanted to pick something up for Molly and the baby.

When they had been talking on the way back to the ship after their shore excursion, he had told her Molly had a baby girl on the fourth of July. No wonder I kept thinking of him that day she thought.

After the shops they went to a trivia game the ship was sponsoring. It was a very laid-back relaxing morning. They both had decided to take advantage of the spa services and had scheduled late morning massages.

It was almost 1:00 p.m. before they went to lunch, and 2:00 p.m. before they stopped to see Miriam. Against doctor's orders she had the I-V removed and was sitting at her desk writing. She looked extremely pale, but at least she was conscious and on her way to recovery.

She thanked Fiona for her concern, but when they asked her if they could stop in again after dinner, she said "no."

"I am fine. There is only one night left, and then we will be home. The doctor has prescribed a sedative. I plan to have an early dinner and go to bed. I will see you two tomorrow morning when we disembark. Now go enjoy yourselves and thank you again for coming to my rescue."

After they left, Fiona turned to Devlin and said, "She still does not look very good but she seems more at peace than I have observed the last few days. She never noticed my ring which is surprising because she always made comments about our jewelry whenever we wore new pieces previously."

"She's been through a lot. Hopefully she will look even better tomorrow. I have a feeling getting off this ship is exactly what she needs."

It seemed strange that evening to see Miriam's empty seat at the dinner table again. They felt like a team with one of their members missing. After Fiona had given everyone the progress report they felt much better, and the conversation became lively. They had a feeling they would never all be simultaneously on the same ship again. It had been a fluke that they had all been invited to be together on a second ship.

"Never say never," Brody said. "You never know. Maybe one of the other ship companies will invite us on a maiden voyage. I sure hope so. I think I can say for all of us that it has been a pleasure working with everyone."

"I totally agree," Peter said. "Any ideas where you two are going for a honeymoon, Fiona?"

"We have not talked about it but I am hoping Devlin wants to go spend some time in the Yucatan Peninsula," she said with a twinkle in her eyes as she looked at him.

"That sounds like a wonderful idea. Maybe we should go for a month."

Fiona rolled her eyes at him, and laughed at what he said.

There was a talent show that evening with cruisers and crew. They all decided since this was their last quality time they could spend with each other they would skip the entertainment, and instead spend their last night at the piano bar.

They were having a wonderful time together when Miriam/Maxine went overboard.

Chapter Forty-Seven

By the time the ship personnel realized Miriam had jumped they knew it was too late to try and save her. Hopefully her body would wash ashore somewhere, but they doubted it.

She had requested a steak dinner that evening, and it was being delivered when the dancer had arrived to relieve the day person. However, Miriam was adamant the girl not stay. She called the doctor, and he reluctantly agreed the woman could leave as long as he could look in on her about 11:00 p.m.

He hated bothering her that late, but he had night duty. She was doing better and had a sedative to help her to get through the last night on board, but he still wanted to check on her. He was surprised when she agreed so quickly without an argument.

So it was a little after 11:00 p.m. when a man on the security staff let the doctor into her cabin. There was a nightlight on, and he entered the bedroom. There was no one in the bed, and it had not been slept in. He checked the bathroom, but there was no sign of life there either. Reentering the living room he saw an envelope propped up on the writing desk. It was addressed to "Zack, the man in the next door suite." The second line read, "Please give this letter to him, if I am not in my room."

The doctor took the note next door. Zack opened the letter and started reading it immediately.

Without finishing reading he looked up and said, "Doctor, I am an insurance investigator, and I am on a case involving the woman next door. I can explain everything in more detail, but right now there is reason to believe she has jumped overboard. Is there a way we can check the cameras for verification?"

It was not long before Zack, the doctor, security, and some ship officers were in the video room reviewing the feed that showed Miriam's balcony. The angle of the camera was much better than on the previous cruise. They clearly saw Miriam without a life jacket talking to herself as she jumped off the balcony from a chair she was standing on. Her arm was raised, and it looked like she had a knife in her hand. Since the time showed 9:10 p.m., over two hours previously, they knew there would be no point in trying to find her. Without a lifejacket there was no way she could stay afloat that long a time.

While they were looking for Miriam on the video feeds, Zack finished reading her letter. He had been shocked, but surprisingly believed what she had written. He was glad she had set the record straight because the way she had acted made so much more sense now. He did feel sworry for what she had suffered.

Zack was not sure if her friends were in their rooms or still out and about. It was almost midnight but he knew he needed to tell them. When he knocked on Devlin's door there was no answer. He then went and knocked on Fiona's door. He heard noise inside and waited for someone to answer the door.

Fiona opened the door in her robe, and Zack saw Devlin coming from the bedroom as he put on his bathrobe. The two of them looked at him with a question in their eyes.

"I hate to bother you this late, but I need to tell you about Miriam."

The two of them looked even more puzzled as he told them about Miriam jumping off her balcony. Fiona was shocked and started crying quietly as he continued his story. He started by telling them he was an insurance investigator, and how Miriam had left him a note to explain her actions.

He had never thought much about multiple personalities, but Fiona nodded as he talked about Miriam/ Maxine. The way she had behaved made so much more sense now. She had even written she suspected her mother had her fiancé killed. Maxine had come to life shortly after he died.

Fiona remembered when Miriam had insisted she was in her hotel all night in Miami when actually she was out with Zack. And she had denied the shopping excursion, when Fiona knew she had seen her. Even though Zack admitted it was he, at the time, he had been too far away for her to get a good look at his face. And Devlin had not gotten a good glimpse of the man the night he had seen them in the nightclub.

So many events now made sense. Even wanting to be called Maxine fit in. At least Miriam had no idea she had killed her mother. However no matter how strong Maxine was, it was not enough to keep the guilt at bay. She had written how her mother had haunted her every night on the cruise to the point she could no longer sleep.

Whenever she looked up when she was in her cabin she would see Emma in a pink prom dress going to the balcony and waving at her while she said, "I am so alone without you. I miss you so much. Please come to me Miriam, please come to me."

In her crazed state she had written to Zack that if

her mother did not stop calling for her; she was going to go mad. She planned to get a knife, and this time she would make sure she killed Emma once and for all. That is why the video showed her jumping off the ship with her hand raised over her head and a knife in it.

"Poor Miriam. I feel so sad for her. What a horrible ending to such an emotionally abused life.

After thanking Zack for telling them about Miriam they went back to bed. However, it was a long time before they could sleep.

The next morning they all disembarked together. Meeting for breakfast, Fiona had told the others about Miriam. Everyone was upset and knew they would never all be together again on another cruise.

Brody had ordered a limo to take them to the airport, and they chatted quietly on the ride there. Since they were all going on the same airline, they were dropped at the same terminal. However, once they got through security they hugged each other and said their good-byes since they had separate flights and different gates.

Devlin had made plans to go to Fiona's house the next day. He wanted to call Molly as soon as he got home to tell his daughter about his engagement. Then he would pack a few things and be on the road to Wisconsin early the next morning. He wanted to start making plans for their wedding as soon as possible, but more importantly he wanted to spend every day with Fiona for the rest of their lives.

As her plane took off Fiona looked at her ring and wondered where the next phase of her life would take her. This last year had been filled with adventures, and she wondered what new escapades would beckon for her and Devlin.

EPILOGUE

It was January 2nd and Fiona and Devlin had just boarded the plane to Cancun for their honeymoon. They would only spend one night there. Renting a car for a month, they planned to explore the Yucatan Peninsula.

They had booked a room in Merida for two weeks to give them time to consider where else they wanted to stay. Campeche was on their list as well as Cozumel. Fiona already had gotten a heads up for an article on the Mayan ruins from her boss.

She spent Thanksgiving and Christmas with Devlin and his family. She felt very welcomed by Molly and her husband, Greg. Fiona knew they would take the place of the children she had never had. She was also enjoying her new role as a grandmother although it had not been official until two days after Christmas.

They had a small wedding with just family and friends. They had been married in Illinois since it was easier for those attending. Fiona had no one she wanted to invite except her friends Kathy and Eric. Diana and Bryan had also come.

"It will give us a chance to explore more of Chicago's attractions," Diana had said when accepting the invitation.

Peter and Brody sadly declined. They had been invited to Spain for the holidays.

The wedding took place at Devlin's church. Molly and Greg had arranged to have the reception at their country club. It was a small affair, but perfect as far as Fiona was concerned.

After spending the last few days with Diana and Bryan, they were now on their way to their honeymoon.

Maxine's shipboard jump had created quite a stir. Because she had suffered so much at the hands of her mother, Zack and his company decided to keep the suicide note private. After all they had been saved from paying the claim, and what would it matter if the world did or did not know that Miriam had a split personality or had killed her mother. She had suffered enough.

Zack felt since the note was addressed to him, Miriam rather Maxine had decided to trust him to do the right thing. They let the press think that the death of her mother had caused her to be so distraught that she had jumped. Since her body was never found, the media attention soon died down.

Miriam had left a will. She had it drawn up after her mother's death when she thought she was coming into a lot of money. The sale of her mother's condo had gone through. Since she had no relatives, she left her estate to the Neuropsychiatric Hospital at UCLA. Maybe someday there would be more help for people like her.

As they disembarked the plane the warm tropical air surrounded them. What a change after the freezing Chicago temperatures. They took a cab to their hotel, and soon they were in their room. As Devlin poured two glasses of the champagne the hotel had provided Fiona went out on the balcony.

The beautiful emerald green of the Caribbean Sea took her breath away. She was glad they had decided to come back to the Yucatan Peninsula for their honeymoon.

As he came up behind her, she heard him say,

"Your life means more to me than anything, Fiona. I love you. There is something I have to tell you. I was so sure of myself when I broke up with you. I feel completely different now. I lived alone for so long, but when I left you, I was lonely. When I saw you at dinner that night on the cruise ship, my heart skipped a beat, and I knew I had to have you in my life forever no matter what it took. My days were so empty without you. I want us to be lovers and best friends forever."

As he pulled her into his arms he realized he had been searching for her his entire life. He just did not realize it until recently.

This was an everlasting love. It was a feeling unhoped for and unexpected. It took total control over them and Fiona understood with total happiness that this was for life.

About the Author

Kileen Prather was born in 1947 in Superior, Wis., and graduated from the University of Wisconsin-Madison with a B.A. in History and a M.A. in School Librarianship from Central Michigan University. Before becoming a writer, she was a school librarian for 21 years and has been a tour manager since 1998. She usually travels in at least 35 states a year and meets wonderful travelers from all over the country who have given her inspiration for her stories. She presently divides her time between Texas and Wisconsin. She is a mother of two boys, Frank & Rick, and grandmother of Isabel.

People who have experienced life over the years are the focus for her books in these modern day romance stories. Their hearts and souls are constantly developing and growing due to the simple fact that they have "lived." The mature reader can relate to the characters' hopes and dreams because of their age, relationships, and experiences. Younger readers can learn what it is like to face life while dealing with its challenges or possibly relate it to someone in their lives.

Her stories take place in various locales in the United States since mature adults have experienced travel, like to travel, or at least dream about going to different places. These characters are ordinary people struggling with issues aging adults have to face such as changing spousal relationships, parental concerns, or illnesses. Many women and men find themselves divorced or widowed after 25, 35, or even 45 years of marriage. These devastating experiences seem to halt life as they know it. They often don't believe it is possible to start over or lead a fulfilling life. They need to know that "living" takes place and "romance is possible" no matter what your age.

Other Books by Kileen Prather

Journey Beckons (available only on Kindle)

Journey to Port

Made in the USA
Monee, IL
27 May 2023

34158446R10164